Copyright

**The unauthorized reproduction or distribution of a
copyrighted work is illegal. Criminal copyright
infringement, including infringement without monetary
gain, is investigated by the FBI and is punishable by fines
and federal imprisonment.**

Please purchase only authorized editions and do not participate in
or encourage, the piracy of copyrighted material. Your support of
author's rights is appreciated.

This book is a work of fiction. Names, characters, places and
incidents are the products of the author's imagination or used
fictitiously. Any resemblance to actual events, locales or persons,
living or dead is entirely coincidental.

The Pact: Syndicate Masters copyrighted 2022 by Delta James

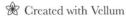

Cover Design: Dar Albert of Wicked Smart Designs

Editing: Bre of Three Point Services

❋ Created with Vellum

THE PACT

SYNDICATE MASTERS

DELTA JAMES

This book is dedicated to my two closest friends—Chris and Renee.
It is also dedicated to The Girls as well as my readers everywhere, who are a constant source of inspiration and support.

Acknowledgements:
Editing: Bre Lockhart, Three Point Author Services
Cover Design: Dar Albert, Wicked Smart Designs

PROLOGUE

$\mathcal{I}$n the dark mists of time, the empire was torn apart by men who valued power over principle. An ancient goddess of courage and honor called upon four great wildcats to become her familiars and impose order on the war-torn realm. Gifting each of them with the ability to shift from beast to man at will, she dispatched them to the four kingdoms: Ireland, Scotland, England, and Wales. As warlords, together they formed the Syndicate to restore all that had been lost.

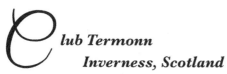

lub Termonn
Inverness, Scotland

Gavan Drummond sat in the lounge of his establishment, Club Termonn. Termonn was Scottish Gaelic for Sanctuary, which was precisely what the club was: his sanctuary. Cat-Sith Castle might be his home and the home of his clan, but as the leader of the clan and the head of the Galloglass Syndicate, his time was rarely his own.

A glass of 100-year-old Macallan single malt rested in his hand and a stunning blonde sat between his legs with her lips wrapped around his cock. He would have preferred it be Kilted Fire single malt, but it was a small distillery, and the current operator had refused his request for distribution, either for his club or to be exported. Blaise Munro was a pain in his ass. Although at some point down the line, he intended to be the one inflicting the pain on her ass. Her grandfather was a good man but had been ill-equipped to raise the fiery-haired beauty. Ach, but it did no good to think about Blaise when Deidre was doing such a good job.

It had been a long day and Gavan wanted to relax. He didn't want to think about Blaise or the ramifications of claiming her but claim her he would. She was, after all, his fated mate.

Gavan had dark hair, dark eyes, and a permanent five o'clock shadow. There was no better way to get his mind to turn off than to settle his six-foot-six muscular frame in a comfortable wingback chair with a beautiful girl giving him a good, long suck. Deidre was a member of his club and was deeply submissive. She found pleasure and satisfaction in servicing many of the Doms in the club.

She licked in long swipes down his staff, swirling her tongue around the head of his cock before sucking it into her mouth. Gavan placed his hand on the back of her head and forced her head down his length. She choked slightly before redoubling her determination to swallow him down. Normally, she offered oral sex to any of the Doms who were interested. She took pride in providing pleasure to the right kind of man and it just so happened that he was that type of man.

Gavan closed his eyes and let her go to town on him, laving the underside of his cock with her tongue.

He closed his fist in her hair to deepen the connection and establish the rhythm he wanted her to use. She moaned, sending the vibrations all along his length, and he could feel his cock swelling.

Deidre didn't try to assert any kind of control when he stilled her head, allowing him to fuck her mouth. He pressed deep, working his way down to the soft, velvety place at the back of her mouth. God, it felt like heaven when she swallowed. As he slid further down her throat, he gave her his cum, shooting it into her belly in a long torrent.

When he finished, he leaned back, enjoying the sensation as she licked him clean before placing his cock back in his leather trousers and lacing him up.

"Better?" he said.

She nodded.

"Good girl." His large hand stroked her hair. "Do you want something to eat or drink?"

Rising gracefully from between his legs, she said, "No, Master Gavan. Thank you again for my session. It really helped."

"All right then but remember that you promised to go home and seek your own bed. No more work for you tonight. If I find you haven't lived up to the terms of our agreement, the next time I see you, it won't be a relaxation session with a flogger you get, but a punishment with my single tail. Agreed?"

She smiled and nodded. Deidre was going to make the sweetest wife and sub for the right Dom someday. And the bastard had better treat her right or he'd answer to Gavan himself. He shook his head as she trotted off to the submissive's salon and locker room.

"Gavan Drummond?" said a small, round man who looked as out of place at the BDSM club as a strumpet would at a church picnic.

"I doubt you'd be standing in my club asking me that if you didn't already know the answer."

The little man pulled his glasses off, then took out a handkerchief and cleaned them before placing them back on his face. Gavan hoped this wasn't going to take long. The little man seemed tightly wound and every time one of the female submissives walked by in fet wear, he looked close to stroking out.

"Yes, well, I suppose that's true enough. I'm Archibald Campbell. I'm Lachlan Munro's solicitor. He gave me your name and said I might be able to contact you here at your club as opposed to traveling to your home on Skye."

"Is there something you found distasteful about either Castle Cat-Sith or Skye?" he said in a menacing tone. He wasn't really angry, but he noticed more and more that Mr. Campbell was having trouble peeling his gaze away from the array of beautiful women who played at Termonn. Perhaps the man would have an easier time dealing with something he was familiar with: a clan leader or mafia boss.

Gavan couldn't fathom anyone not wanting to at

least visit, if not live, on the Isle of Skye. In his mind, it was the most beautiful place in all the world, and he'd seen a great many places in the world. It was a place given to wild storms that struck with the ferocity of a feral tiger, but always gave way to a clear, cloudless blue sky. It was said that if you'd been born there, a part of you would always remain; its rapture ran through your veins. The tempestuous elements combined with its breathtaking beauty would be an integral part of your soul forever. He might conduct most of his business here in Inverness, but Skye was home.

"I-uhm-I find nothing wrong with either your castle or the island itself. It's just that I-uhm-I'm not used to such fine things," he stuttered, gesturing to his surroundings.

"Beautiful women who choose not to hide their loveliness? A comfortable club that caters to the needs of its members with good food, better spirits, and marvelous companions? Then you should frequent better establishments." Gavan was playing with the man, much like a cat did with its food.

"If the matter were not so urgent nor so dire, I would have waited until tomorrow and contacted you for an appointment."

"Then sit Mr. Campbell. Can I get you a drink or something to eat?" offered Gavan.

"I could use a spot of good whisky and maybe a wee bite to eat."

Gavan gestured to one of the servers. "Bring Mr. Campbell some of my private stock and a selection of our appetizers." The server smiled and went to do his bidding. "So, Mr. Campbell, what is it you wish to discuss?"

"You have had some dealings, legal ones, with Mr. Munro." He worded the sentence both like a question and a statement.

Gavan nodded. "Contrary to popular belief, the vast majority of my business is all very legal."

Campbell shook his head. "How do you know I'm not with Scotland Yard or Interpol or any number of other legal entities?"

"Simple. I make it my business to know those who enter my club. The moment you walked through those doors, my head of security ran your face through our photo recognition and identification system against operatives of all kinds, even the ones who don't appear on any official roster. If you were a copper, you'd have been tossed out long before you ever got to me."

"I'm not sure if you're aware, but Mr. Munro is gravely ill."

"I'm sorry to hear that." Time to shake the little solicitor up. "He was one of the first members of the club when I opened it."

"Lachlan Munro was a member of this establishment?" Campbell said with equal parts shock and disdain.

"Exactly what kind of establishment do you think I'm running?"

Gavan knew precisely what kind of business Campbell thought he was running. Unlike his compatriot in Ireland, Gavan wasn't above running a business for prostitutes in his territory. The difference between he and most other mafia types was that it was done more for the protection of those who sold sex for a living than for his own profit. He didn't tolerate coercion or kidnapping. More than one human trafficker had found himself dead and tossed into the unforgiving waters of the North Atlantic.

"I'm sure that's not my concern," he stammered.

"It isn't at all, but just for your information, this club is not a brothel, nor do we offer sex-for-sale. Termonn is a lifestyle, kink, BDSM club or dungeon, depending on which vernacular you prefer. Everything done here, everything, is consensual between adults."

"I am not unaware of your club or the activities you and your patrons engage in, but I find it difficult to believe that any woman would choose to be abused."

"You're a *fandan*. No one is abused. Some submissives find pain and dominance enhance their sexual experience and afford them solace they can find nowhere else. Most dominants find the same thing with having control." Gavan ticked off the most common misconceptions about the lifestyle. "And not all submissives are female. Termonn does not discriminate."

"A man submitting to a woman is unnatural."

Gavan laughed. "I'd be very careful spouting that bullshite in my club, Campbell. I have several badass Dommes who'd like nothing better than to take some chauvinistic misogynist to task and bend him to her will. I'd also watch that judgmental shit around Lachlan Munro."

Gavan wasn't about to tell the little worm that his client was a submissive of the first order and had only found his real peace when he'd figured out who he was and what he wanted. It was difficult enough for a man to admit he was a Dom. He imagined admitting he was a sub would be even harder. Most vanilla types, and even some familiar with the lifestyle, were loath to admit it. In Gavan's experience, it was those men who were deeply submissive who avoided the lifestyle like the plague and, like Campbell, eschewed the notion that such a thing was even possible.

"Mr. Munro's lifestyle choices are not of my concern. He is free to live any way he chooses."

"Well, then, at least we're in agreement about that. So, Campbell, what is it you want? I was feeling nice and relaxed after Diedre sucked me off, but you're starting to annoy me, which I'm sure you've deduced isn't typically a good thing."

"This is a delicate matter," Campbell started.

"Look around you. Here in the lounge, there are

people in various stages of undress, some are completely nude. Some subs sit in their Dom's lap, while others rest between their legs with their head on their Dom's thigh. The couple standing at the bar are negotiating a scene. My guess is the woman is looking to be bound and tickled before she has intercourse. The good news is the Dom is one of our shibari masters and has a real fetish for sensation play of all kinds. Most likely when they leave here tonight, both will be in a much better, more relaxed, sated and happy state of mind and body. People are starting to pick up on your judgmental attitude and it's messing with the vibe. I'm beginning to wish I'd never allowed you into my club."

Before he could decide whether or not he wanted to toss the little pipsqueak out into the cold night, Hamish MacLeod, his second in command, approached them. Hamish had been with him for years. They'd been in Special Ops before returning to Skye and forming the Galloglass Syndicate. Hamish was six-foot-three and almost sixteen stone of pure muscle. His ability to move quickly and quietly belied his physicality.

"Gav, I hate to break up the party, but there's a situation. Gere needs to speak to you in your office."

Gavan turned to Campbell. "It seems your time is up, Campbell. I think it's best we finish the discussion at Castle Cat-Sith in the morning. My driver will be by for you at nine tomorrow. Upon arrival, you'll have thirty minutes to tell me what it is you need. Feel free to finish your drink and the food." He turned to the bartender. "Malcolm, see that Mr. Campbell is escorted from the club when he's finished."

"Mr. Drummond, I really do need to talk to you about a business matter."

"Then you shouldn't have wasted my time being a judgmental prick." Gavan turned to leave.

"Mr. Drummond..." the solicitor's voice bordered on strident. "It's imperative I pass along this information."

Gavan closed the space between them. "Then speak quickly, Campbell. If Hamish says I have urgent business, then I need to see to it."

"Mr. Munro needs to speak with you at your earliest convenience, tomorrow if at all possible."

Something about the way Campbell delivered the message got through to Gavan and he eyed the solicitor speculatively. "I've known Lachlan a long time. Why is he sending a solicitor to tell me he needs to see me?"

Campbell dropped his voice. "I'm afraid Mr. Munro's health has become dire."

"Tell him I'll be round to the house at eight. If that isn't convenient, call the club and leave a better time with anyone who answers. They'll see that the message gets to me."

Pushing concern for the old man aside, he went to deal with whatever the hell Gere and Hamish were concerned about. Nothing good had ever come from something his second and his lieutenant in Inverness were concerned about. As he jogged up the steps with Hamish on his heels, he couldn't help but wonder what the next few days might bring.

CHAPTER 2

*K*ilted Fire Distillery
Isle of Skye, Scotland

Blaise Munro awoke to the smell of smoke and rolled out of bed. Pulling on her jeans, but only sitting down long enough to tuck them into her cowboy boots, she rushed to the window as she pulled on a bra and threw a sweater over her head. Smoke billowed out of the building furthest from the house. *Fire!* Before she could open the window and sound the alarm, the large bell kept at the entrance to the still-house began to clang. Long ago her family had installed alarm bells, each with a distinct tone so that when someone rang it, everyone within ear shot would know the location of the fire.

Grabbing a knit ski cap and scarf, she ran down the stairs and towards the front door. Vera, her grand-father's caretaker, came out of his room.

"Tell Granda I'm on my way out. As soon as I know what it is, I'll be back to let you know."

"Should I be worried about moving him?"

"No. The alarm bell is for the stillhouse. Regardless of what it is, I'm sure you're safe enough here. If not, I'll send someone to help you."

Vera nodded, but said nothing before turning to go back inside. Blaise was halfway to the stillhouse when she saw her assistant Tommy's car coming down the drive. She glanced at her watch; Tommy was early. Normally they didn't get started until eight o'clock and Tommy usually skated in just under the wire.

She tossed her curly red mane, which fell past her shoulders, back over her head before donning the cap and scarf. Her stormy green eyes, normally tranquil, blazed with emotion and concern. She could see Tommy rushing toward the building from his car. At just under six feet, he wasn't that much taller than Blaise. His blond hair and angelic face would have been a magnet for almost any woman, only Tommy wasn't geared that way.

"Fuck me," she muttered to herself.

If it wasn't one thing, it was another and now her grandfather's health had taken a turn for the worse and Gavan Drummond was supposed to be paying them a visit. What the hell did the leader of the Gallowglass Syndicate want with them? She'd refused his request to supply his lifestyle club with their single malt scotch. Did the arrogant prick think he could go around her to her grandfather? It wouldn't work and she meant to disabuse him of any notion to the contrary.

She'd known Gavan Drummond almost from the moment her grandfather had brought her home to the Isle of Skye after her parents died. He and her grandfather had, what she called an adversarial friendship, On one hand, they seemed to like and respect each other; on the other, they kept a wary eye out. Not that she would mind keeping an eye on Drummond; he was easy on the eyes, after all. Tall with a muscular frame, dark hair, dark eyes, and permanent dark stubble. She'd seen him in leathers once when he visited Baker Street, and he'd been like a god among men. Her friend JJ, who owned Baker Street, had once described her first meeting with her now Dom and husband, Robert Fitzwallace, as having left her gobsmacked. Seeing Drummond in his black leather trousers riding low on his hips, exposing his cut chest, eight-pack abs, and those sexy hip notches had left her feeling the same way.

He'd wielded a single-tail whip in a manner that had left the sub bound to a St. Andrew's Cross crying out again and again in repeated ecstasy. When she'd finally sagged against it, Drummond had taken extreme care with her, releasing her from her restraints and providing her with aftercare that had been hypnotic in its gentleness. From that point forward, Blaise's fantasies had increasingly featured the Scottish Dom. However, the idea of submitting to him in the real world was just not something she'd do. She had no intention of becoming involved with some mafia boss.

The last thing she needed on top of everything else was anything that had to do with Lord Gavan Drummond of Castle Cat-Sith, the Galloglass Syndicate, or Club Termonn.

"What the hell happened, Tommy?" she said as she rushed toward the stillhouse.

"I don't bloody well know. I just got here," he answered, running behind her and trying to keep up.

Thick black smoke poured from the main doors. *What could have caused the fire?* Blaise had checked the fires beneath the stills herself last night. They'd been properly banked so that there would be no chance they could flare back into an open flame. While the stills had ventilation systems that kept ash and smoke out of her workers' lungs, the fire itself was still exposed. Plenty of distilleries had gone to either steam jackets around or steam coils inside their pot stills, but Kilted Fire still used an open flame fueled and stoked by coal. If smoke was being forced out the door, then something had gone terribly wrong.

"Fire gear!" she yelled, pulling her own over her head as she tucked the edges of the hood and her hair beneath the opening of her sweater. "Nobody goes back inside without the proper equipment."

Full face masks with respirators and hoods were issued to everyone at the distillery. Breathing the noxious ash or smoke from a coal fire could be as life-threatening as the flames themselves.

"I'm going to find the source. Check each still in order and deal with any problems," she shouted to Tommy. "Half of you come with me. Split the rest in two. One group with Tommy, the rest outside to check for any sign of other flames.

Blaise ran into the smoke filled stillhouse. Black smoke seemed to be everywhere, but the heat wasn't as intense as she'd feared it would be. She'd pulled on her firefighter gloves, another item issued to every worker, as she ran. Kilted Fire had an excellent safety record and for more than two centuries it had put its workers first. That dedication to their staff had cost them dearly on more than one occasion and had even put them on the brink of disaster once.

From the time she'd joined him at fifteen, her granda had drilled into her that their people came first, their stills came second and everything else was a distant third. Blaise bit back the tears that threatened to erupt. Her granda had been a powerful force in her life. When her parents had been killed in a ferry accident between Skye and the mainland, it had been her granda who'd brought her home.

She hadn't known him then because her parents hadn't spoken of him. Her mother and father had married against their parents' wishes and had only recently started to try repairing the relationship with her mother's father, the indomitable Lachlan Munro. When the ferry sank, only ten survivors were pulled from the icy water, but Blaise had been among them. Her granda hadn't even hesitated and had laid claim to her. When she'd turned eighteen, she'd petitioned the court to change her last name to Munro.

As the thoughts from the past floated away, she was pulled back to the present and realized that the long length of the distillery was of no help to her now. She had to find the source of the flames. Tommy would have to check the integrity and safety of the other stills. The closer she got to Still 1, the more intense the heat became. By the time she reached Still 2, the smoke all but engulfed her. The fire no longer sizzled, but rather crackled as sparks flew from beneath the still. The blaze tried to bully her back as it attempted to greedily consume everything it could. The situation was going from chaotic to disaster almost faster than her brain could process.

Blaise felt a hand on her shoulder and tried to knock it away. Any of her people would let go. Instead, the hand gripped her tighter.

"We're getting out of here, Blaise. Scottish Fire and Rescue has been called. It's too dangerous for you in here," barked a voice that was all too familiar. Gavan Drummond had arrived.

Blaise whirled around, dislodging Drummond's grip on her. She turned back and headed toward Still

1. If she could get to it, she could shut off the air supply to the coal, which would, in theory, reduce, if not extinguish, the flame. She was almost there when the hand clamped down on her shoulder again.

"Now, Blaise!" he roared over the flames.

Who the fuck did this eejit think he was? "Let go and get out," she shouted.

The mountain of a man swore, and she couldn't hear what he mumbled after, but she was pretty sure he said something about a spanking. *God, she needed some time off.* She'd been increasingly horny for months. The problem was that the Isle of Skye was a small community, and the closest kink club was one her grandfather played at. He didn't think she knew, but she did and didn't think less of him for it. However, the idea of running into her grandfather there kind of turned her stomach.

Blaise knew that for a lot of subs, submission was a response to some kind of trauma or trying to fix what had been missing for them. The only way they could enjoy sex was if they felt it was forced upon them or that they'd unwillingly given over to a Dom. Such was not the case for her. She was geared to respond only to a truly dominant alpha male who understood that it was just for sex and that she would never be anyone's slave. Calling a partner "Master" had always been a hard limit for her. Pain, by itself, did little to nothing for her. But voluntarily relinquishing control for a few hours set her free and allowed her to fly. Blaise needed a Dom to get out of her own head, if only for a little while.

Drummond's hand reached out and spun her around. She didn't have time to react, she didn't have time to think, and she barely had time to breathe before she was hauled close to his muscular body and hoisted over his shoulder as if her weight was nothing. As he turned to run out of the stillhouse, she saw her people were coming toward them with the firehose, and she could hear the sounds of the fire engines closing in. They should be able to put the fire out easily. If the bastard whose clavicle she was now bouncing on as he ran had let her be, she'd have had the damn thing out before the people from the Fire and Rescue Service ever got out of their vehicles.

What was Drummond thinking? Who did he think he was, turning that smooth as good whisky voice on her? That wasn't really a question, though. Gavan Drummond, the titular lord of Castle Cat-Sith, thought he bloody well ran the Isle of Skye as his personal fiefdom. Maybe he did, but he didn't run Kilted Fire or her.

The Drummonds had held at least part of the Isle of Skye for centuries, just not as much of the isle nor for as long as Clans MacDonald, MacKinnon, and MacLeod. And it had been the Drummonds who'd moved in, got a toe-hold on the island, then masterfully played the other clans against each other until only Castle Cat-Sith remained.

His business interests on Skye notwithstanding, Drummond also had business interests in Inverness, including owning Club Termonn. Additionally, he was reputed to be the head of the Galloglass Syndicate, the largest and most dangerous mafia group in all of Scotland. It was said that if Gavan Drummond wanted you dead, you'd best dig your own grave and pay for your own funeral.

Once they were well away from the stillhouse, he set her down next to his vintage Range Rover. She dragged the fire hood from her head just as the Fire and Rescue vehicles came barreling down the long drive. Their response time was improving. She turned and looked toward the stillhouse. Her people had done their jobs; the difference in the color and smell of the smoke told her they had it under control. The Fire and Rescue Service hadn't been needed after all.

"Have you lost your mind?" growled Drummond as he pulled the fire hood from his own head. "Didn't you hear me when I told you Fire and Rescue was on the way and you didn't need to risk your life?"

"I wasn't in any danger until you saw fit to interfere. You'll notice my people got the fire extinguished. I could have done that even sooner if you hadn't stuck your nose in where it doesn't belong."

Drummond pulled his hand down his face in a show of exasperation. It looked as though he was trying to rein in his temper, which was odd as he was known as an iceman in certain circles, famous for remaining cool under pressure and always being in command of any given situation. His power and control were absolute, and no one, from the subs and other Doms in his club to his mafia rivals and Scotland Yard, dared defy him.

"Ye daft girl," he said, his brogue thickening considerably. "The whole thing could have gone up in flames. God knows there was enough fuel in the damn place."

"This may come as a shock to you Lord Drummond..."

"So, you did recognize me."

"You'd be surprised what a daft girl like me knows," snarled Blaise.

The man was infuriating. Six and a half feet of pure muscle and alpha attitude. He truly fit the age-old description of tall, dark, and handsome; only, Blaise would have substituted lethal for handsome. It wasn't that he wasn't good looking, he was, but Blaise could sense the smoldering predatory nature of the man even when he was trying to cover it up.

The man was drool worthy. His chest was covered in dark hair that had a pleasure trail running down to his washboard abs and disappearing below the waist of his trousers. She'd been fairly certain the enormous bulge behind his fly hadn't been a weapon. Well, rumor had it that it was indeed a weapon, just not a gun.

"I told you to leave it..." he started to say.

"I'm not accustomed to taking orders from you or any other man."

He took a deep breath, expelling it in a sigh. His strong hand reached out to tuck an errant strand of her hair behind her ear. "I think you'd enjoy taking orders from the right man."

"Unfortunately for you, you will never know. Now, if you'll excuse me, I need to see to my people, my distillery, and speak to the Fire and Rescue squad. I assume you called them?"

"Yes, I could see the smoke. I was a bit surprised that no one else had called."

"Because we didn't need their help. If there's a penalty fee for calling them when they weren't needed, I'll make sure they send you the bill. Why the hell are you down here at the works anyway? My grandfather is up in the house. And why does he want to see you exactly?"

"I have no idea. Your grandfather's solicitor relayed a message that your grandfather wanted an audience, so here I am."

Blaise glanced down at her watch. "It isn't even eight o'clock." It wasn't much before eight, but still, it seemed awfully early for a casual meeting. What the hell was her grandfather up to?

"I've known your granda for a long time, and I know he's an early riser. If he sent Campbell to my club to track me down, it's important."

"Then you'd best go meet with him, but when

you're done, Drummond, I want you off our land. I don't need you and all the trouble that comes with you tarnishing my good name or sullying the reputation of Kilted Fire."

She shoved his chest, moving him out of her way, before heading for the stillhouse. It took every ounce of willpower not to look back over her shoulder. Insulting and trading barbs with Gavan Drummond was not a wise thing to do, and yet tugging the tiger's tail seemed to be just the thing she needed to restore equanimity to her morning. Tiger? That did seem to suit him: beautiful to look at, but dangerous to play with.

CHAPTER 3

*I*t was a good thing Gavan had so much respect and affection for the old man. If not, he'd have been tempted to hoist the wild spitfire back over his shoulder, find a quiet place, and put her over his knee. If any female ever needed a spanking, it was Blaise Munro. There wasn't a man on the Isle of Skye who dared cross her. She had a quick and sharp wit that she could back up with boxing skills he was sure her grandfather had taught her.

When he'd seen her name on the guest sheet for Termonn, he'd told the staff she was to be treated with every courtesy. Somehow she'd found out her grandfather was a member and had withdrawn her application, but not before Gavan had a chance to see her list of interests as well as hard and soft limits. When he'd found out she'd begun to frequent Baker Street, he'd tried to arrange a meeting, which had proven unsuccessful so far. Maybe it was time to call in a favor with Robert Fitzwallace. Fitz and his wife/sub, JJ, owned Baker Street.

Gavan had never had any interest in taking a full-time sub, much less marrying one, but from the time he'd seen Blaise tricked out in a forest green with black lace trim corset and black leather boy shorts, he'd begun to rethink that decision. She called to him in a way that no other had. Strong, smart, provocative, and gorgeous, he'd wanted a ring on her finger and a collar around her throat. He'd even gone so far as to have both custom-made for her. *Enjoy your freedom, my little wildcat. Your days of not answering to a man's authority are coming to an end.* Depending on the state of Lachlan's health, he might ask the old man for his blessing today.

As he'd said to Blaise, he and her grandfather had known each other and each other's secrets for a very long time. Lachlan had come to his aid one night when a rival syndicate had thought to take him out. Gavan had only survived due to his superior physiology. Lachlan had found him gravely wounded down by the seashore and had dragged him home to tend his wounds and nurse him back to health.

Gavan remembered watching Lachlan watch over him as he feigned sleep through hooded eyes.

"There's no need to do that, lad," the old man said. "I know you're awake."

"I'm a little old for you to be calling me lad," rebuked Gavan.

"When yer as old as I am, everybody is young by comparison. Besides which, I know who and what you are. The Munros of Kilted Fire have served the Drummonds of Cat-Sith for centuries. As far as I'm concerned, there's no need to stop now. I haven't called yer people as I had no idea whether you were betrayed by one of your own."

Gavan shook his head. "Never."

"Do ye know if it was one of your own kind or someone from the wrong side of the law?"

"What do you mean my own kind?"

"Ye know damn good and well what I mean. As I say, the Munros have served the Drummonds for a very long time. We have held to our pledge to keep your secrets and we will continue to do so."

Gavan realized he was on the cusp of insulting the man who had, in all likelihood, saved his life. "I'm a suspicious bastard by nature. I apologize for my less than grateful attitude. And I am grateful. If ever I can be of help to you and yours, you only have to ask."

That had been shortly before Lachlan's granddaughter had come to live with him. Gavan had never thought to take over leadership of the clan or the syndicate at such an early age. By the time Lachlan had nursed him back to health, he was twenty-three and already had enemies twice as old as he was, but only half as lethal.

In the subsequent years, not once had Lachlan asked him for his assistance. Granting him privileges at Termonn had been easy enough to do, especially as he was sure the old man knew it was Gavan's club. Some of the assistance Gavan had given had been more delicate and had taken a gentle hand, things like ensuring loan requests got approved and keeping the Scottish Crime and Drug Enforcement Agency or SCDEA away from not only his own smuggling operations but those of Kilted Fire. Gavan had been surprised to discover Lachlan's illegal contraband: peat from the Highlands.

The peat fields on the Kilted Fire estate had all but given out, and the peatlands on Skye had wanted to charge him more than the old man wanted to pay. He'd begun smuggling peat in from the Highlands. The illegal sourcing of peat hadn't lasted long because Blaise began to restore and reclaim Kilted Fire's own fields. She had the knowledge and determination to ensure that they could supply their own peat for years to come. Blaise had also struck a deal with one of the last family-owned coal mines to buy the fuel she needed for her stills.

The old man had laid one hell of a burden on his granddaughter, and she'd risen to the challenge. No wonder she needed the peace and freedom that came with submitting, at least sexually, to a Dom. If Gavan had his way, she'd find there was even more to be had, including being loved, cherished, and protected if she gave over completely to the right Dom. One of the things she'd listed as being curious about was suspension play. He could see where that would appeal to her. He hoped that she had yet to experience that as he'd love to show her just how liberating being bound and suspended could be. In fact, now that he thought about it, the idea of another man playing with her made his blood boil.

Gavan watched her return to the stillhouse and forced himself to turn toward the main house. He hadn't overstated his concern about what Lachlan might want. From her face and her body language, he rather imagined Blaise didn't know either. Climbing the steps to the massive front door, he used the knocker to request entry.

"Good morning, Gavan," said Vera, Lachlan's companion and Domme.

Gavan wondered if anyone could guess the depth of their commitment to one another. "Good morning, Vera. I take it Campbell passed on the information and that this doesn't impose too much stress on Lachlan's health."

Seeing the proud, strong Domme's face begin to crack, he reached for her, but she brushed him aside. "Lachlan is waiting to see you. Please listen to all he has to say before rejecting his proposal, and don't tell him you saw me start to break down."

"Just because you're the Domme," said Gavan

gently, "it doesn't mean you have to go through whatever this is alone. Care to share what that might be?"

"Only because I know you care for and understand him. He's not unaware of the assistance you have provided him over the years and has always been grateful for your discretion, but he means to take you up on the debt you believe you still owe him." She paused and drew a deep breath. "He's dying, Gavan, and there's nothing the doctors, you, or I can do to stop it."

Gavan nodded. "I thought that might be what this is about. I don't just think I owe him, I know I do. As he pointed out to me, the Munros have served the Drummonds for centuries. All that I have done before was done because of that alliance. What I do for him now is in payment of any remaining debt."

"You're a good man, Lord Gavan Drummond, and don't you believe for one minute that those in your territory don't know the power and influence you use to keep us safe and provide for your people." She patted his arm.

"Does he know about the fire?"

"Aye. He smelled the smoke. As soon as I told him Blaise was headed down to the works, he settled."

"Ach, she never should have gone into that stillhouse, nor should the other workers."

"Our people know what's at stake, and the family has provided training and equipment. Blaise would never have put her people in danger. It's a trait the two of you share."

Gavan could see no reason to argue as they moved across the room. He didn't doubt that Blaise cared for her people, but he did wonder who was caring for Blaise.

"I take it the fire is out. What caused it?" asked Lachlan in a far stronger voice than Gavan had been expecting. As they entered the new space, Vera left them alone.

"Not sure what caused it, but Blaise seemed to think it was one of the stills."

"Hmm. I might need you to check into it on the sly."

"You don't think it was an accident?"

Lachlan laughed. "No. The last thing Blaise does before she goes to bed is check the stills. Mind you, if she had the right man waiting for her in her bed, she might be willing to delegate that task."

Gavan laughed. "Somehow I don't think you sent that *fandan* to see me to talk about the state of Blaise's sex life."

"Nay. But he's such a pretentious little prick I thought you might find him amusing. I will say that he's good at his job, which kind of makes him the annoying sod that he is."

Lachlan might be dying, but the old man hadn't lost his sense of humor. "Why have you called me?" Gavan said formally, feeling it might make it easier on

Lachlan to ask whatever it was that was weighing on him.

"I suspect Vera told you I was dying. It's going to be hard on Blaise, mostly because I didn't want her burdened with that knowledge. She's going to want some fancy funeral that costs way too much money. I don't mind that if it'll get her through, but I want you to gather my friends and workers and throw a party in my honor. Lots of good food, laughter, and Kilted Fire scotch. I want people to share stories and jokes, things from our pasts, and plans for our future. Can you handle that?"

"Aye. You know I will. What else?"

"Look after Vera for me. I know she's the Domme and she thinks that means she has to handle everything alone. You're a Dom, so she'll listen to you when you tell her that isn't how it works. She's going to need someone to lean on. She once told me she thought you were the best Dom she'd ever known."

Gavan nodded. "Done."

"And last, take care of Blaise. She thinks she's like this island: alone, impenetrable, and strong. She needs the right Dom to show her the strength that true submission takes along with the peace and solace she could find in it. She needs someone to take care of her and to love her. Will you do that for me?"

Why he'd thought before now that the old man wouldn't know his feelings for Blaise were beyond him. Lachlan Munro was nobody's fool. "Aye. I have no doubt that you already know that as far as Blaise is concerned, the only reason I've never claimed her as mine was my respect for you."

"I know," he said quietly. "I've seen the way you looked at her for years, always keeping a watchful eye. But selfishly, I didn't want to share her with you. Then, I hoped she'd figure it out on her own, but it's too late for me now to push her in your direction. So know, Gavan Drummond, that you have my blessing."

"I'm not sure in this day and age that I can force her hand."

"Aye, I've thought about that, and I may have come up with a way to help…"

"Lachlan, I've told you before, you're not to interfere."

"Aye, but I wasn't dying before, Gavan. I need to know she's going to be safe."

"You have my word on that."

"Hear me out lad—it's a beauty of a plan," said the old man, his eyes shining with mischief,

An hour later, Gavan had set Lachlan's mind at ease and left. He doubted he would ever see the old man again and was sorry for it. He had to agree that Lachlan's plan was deceptively simple and devious as hell. No wonder he liked it. Lachlan's dying wish had given Gavan all he needed to claim Blaise Munro as his own, regardless of her initial feelings on the matter.

After Gavan Drummond of Castle Cat-Sith and Club Termonn had left, Vera returned to the room and joined the old man.

"I won't like what you've set in motion, will I?" she asked.

"Probably not, but I daresay you'll like it more than Blaise will… at least at first," answered Lachlan Munro with a gleam in his eye.

"What have you done?" she whispered.

"What needed to be done to ensure your and Blaise's safety, as well as the continuation of the distillery and Drummond's line. He's been in love with her for years and her with him, but the bloody bastard made me promise not to interfere, so I didn't. I've watched the two of them dance around and avoid one another until I wanted to puke. I should never have listened to him when he threatened me."

"The man is with the mafia, Lachlan."

Lachlan chuckled softly, taking her hands in his. "He is so much more than that, so very much more."

CHAPTER 4

*G*avan drove back to Castle Cat-Sith. It was old, not perhaps as old as other castles that had fallen to ruin, but old enough to have been built as a formidable fortress along the coast of the Isle of Skye. His kind and his family had pulled back from the mainland when they'd feared for the lives of those they held dear. Castle Cat-Sith could withstand a siege and offered more than one way to get the women and children to safety in case of an attack. It was also isolated and remote, thus affording his clan the freedom to shift between their human and altered selves.

He pulled up in front of the castle and one of the car jockeys came out to see to his vehicle. Hamish greeted him as he entered the great hall, then followed him into Gavan's study and closed the door behind them.

"Was it as you feared, Gav? The old man is dying?"

"He is. He called in his marker."

"His marker? For Christ's sake, Gav. You have repaid that debt many times over."

"Have I?" asked Gavan with a quirked brow. "How does one repay a man for saving his life and never betraying the secrets of his true nature or that of his clan?"

Hamish nodded. "Point taken. So what did he want? And did you tell him how you felt about his granddaughter?"

"What do you mean by that?"

"Gav, there's not a one of us here at the castle or the club or in Inverness or in the Syndicate that doesn't know how you feel. You've been obsessed with her since the day you met her and as far as I know, you haven't fucked a woman in years."

"There are an awful lot of subs who would tell you differently."

"Only if they're lying. Oh, I think you took care of their needs, getting them off numerous times in a session and you've allowed them to suck you dry, but not once have you gotten between a woman's legs and hammered her until you filled her pussy with your cum. Not once have you listened to her yowl as you score her cunt, preparing her for your seed. Look me in the eye and tell me I'm wrong." Gavan said nothing. "Exactly. So did he give you his blessing?"

Gavan nodded as a slow smile spread across his face. "Aye, he did just that and has even hatched a plan to help. But as I have just seen Lachlan alive for what is likely to be the last time and had a frustrating interaction with Blaise which scared the shit out of me—she literally ran into a burning building—and have now had to confirm your lewd opinions of my sorry state, I'm going for a run."

Gavan shooed Hamish out, then removed his clothes before calling for his great beast. The black tiger was there, always waiting, always watching. As the light became distorted and refracted, it shimmered all around him. He could see the animal in his mind's eye. As it galloped toward him, it leapt with a great roar, initiating the change, and taking control of Gavan's body.

He craned his head and stretched his body, flexing all of his muscles before pushing the hidden button with his snout to open the secret door that led to one of the Castle's many escape routes. There were miles and miles of tunnels under the castle. It was entirely possible for someone to get lost and die without ever seeing the light of day again.

The passageways were always a bit damp, but Gavan thought they were dry enough. As the castle's grounds bordered the ocean and many of the escape routes led to the sea, a number of them could be flooded at any time. But not today. Today the tunnels had hard-packed sand and were filled with the smell of the sea. The ocean beckoned to him. There were times he was almost surprised that he wasn't a shark-shifter or orca-shifter because the call to be close to the clear blue deep water that lay just offshore was so strong.

Gavan charged down the corridors beneath the castle, always following his nose as it drew him forward. The only scent sweeter, was hers. He longed to sniff, taste, and touch every inch of Blaise Munro, and now he would have the means to do it. He would try and court her at first, use his powers of persuasion, but if that didn't work, he'd simply revert to his more primitive side and claim what was his. He was sure that once he had her in his bed long enough and had turned her, she would succumb and revel in his embrace. Gavan would give her everything...whether she wanted it or not.

The thought of Blaise's reaction to having to truly submit to his authority and being punished when she stepped too far out of line was enticing and incredibly arousing. It was easy for him to imagine her face down over his knee, pinned in place as he rained his discipline down on her sumptuous buttocks. He could almost hear her cries of angry indignation turning to capitulation as she surrendered to his authority and the color of her flesh turned from ivory to pink to red.

Running down the steep incline, he noticed the walls were wetter as was the hard-pack sand he ran along. This part of the escape system filled with water on a regular basis. He burst out into the open sunlight and roared, the sound filling the air and reverberating off the walls of the craggy cliffs. Castle Cat-Sith was remote enough that the only ones who could hear him were his own people.

He charged down the beach, weaving in and out of the stormy seas and splashing in the cold water, not only to play but to see if he could ease the growing fire in his blood. So far, it was not having the desired effect, but it felt good, nonetheless. Plunging into the icy water, he swam to a promontory rock he liked to use to watch those who came to celebrate the clan's monthly bonfire nights, Oidhche Teine, or just Teine.

The bonfires were a way for his people to recon-nect on a regular basis not only with one another and their clan leader, but with the land and the nature of their kind. Wrestling matches and rough play were commonplace, and often the sound of his clan's tigresses' satisfied yowling could be heard from outside the glow of the fire.

Only matched pairs were allowed to participate in the breeding ritual. A male tiger would mount a willing female from behind, grasp the nape of her neck and allow the barbs that covered his cock to unfold as he thrust in and out, scraping and preparing her pussy for his cum. In order to conceive, a female had to be in estrus, but most tigers enjoyed the ritual regardless of whether they were trying to get preg-nant. Unmated pairs did without—no excuses, no second chances. They might have sex, but a man was expected to keep his barbs only to himself and his mate. The breaking of that fundamental tenant would get one or both of the participants banished from the clan.

Teine would soon be upon them. It was custom for newly mated pairs to attend and to be heard as the male claimed his mate fully for the first time. The fact that Lachlan had shared with him that Blaise knew nothing of their kind was somewhat problematic, but not something he couldn't overcome. Gavan would simply need to turn her before the next Teine, then he could honor the ancient ways of their people while satisfying his heart's desire.

The swim in the frigid water had done little to satiate his rising need for her. Usually, when anywhere in her proximity, he simply endured the way his cock misbehaved. It grew hard and painful way past the pharmaceutical companies' warnings about Viagra. Hamish had been right; it had been years since he'd had a woman beneath him, and never had he let his barbs come out to play.

Maybe a swim back in his human form, coupled with a walk along the windy beach and a run back to the castle would calm his recalcitrant cock, but he rather doubted it. Regardless, it was worth trying. Gavan forced the tiger to recede, called forth his humanity and dove under the white-capped waves before moving back to shore with a strong, sure stroke.

Once on land, he shook himself off and let the wind do the rest. He trekked along the remainder of the shoreline of their private cove before running up to the dune line where the sand was deeper and softer, then he turned for home.

Once he entered the tunnels, he thought about going back to his study to pick up his wool trousers and white linen shirt but decided against it. Instead, he went up to his chambers to take a shower and redress. Lachlan had given him a lot to think about and had possibly provided the key to fulfilling Gavan's deepest wishes.

Damn the man! Why did Gavan Drummond have such a profound effect on her? There was a time when she'd been wildly attracted to the man. That wasn't technically true. Physically, he still had a way to arouse her as no other man ever had. He'd also filled her teenage and young woman's fantasies. Past tense wasn't applicable to that either. He still did. It was rare that she didn't fantasize that it was Gavan's strong hands and powerful cock that pounded her pussy again and again, forcing orgasm after orgasm from her.

Blaise shook her head. The fantasies she had about Gavan were powerful and disturbing. She tried to have vanilla fantasies when handling herself or tried to recall various scenes and sexual encounters she'd had, but lately they'd frustrated her more than they'd helped. Sub drop had become a given after any scene. She tried to tell herself it was normal and had nothing to do with Gavan, but she knew better.

There had been a time she'd been able to scene with a partner, get a release, have sex and go on her way, but she rarely played more than twice with any man. After a while, having intercourse with someone had seemed wrong when it was Gavan she craved. Instead, she'd relied on the scene—flogging, wax play, etc.—to get her off before she provided her partner with a blow job. She had mad skills with oral sex, and she was always up front that it was the only thing she was offering. More often than not, she left the club with more stress and frustration than when she'd gone in. Several Doms had offered to help her sort through her feelings, but she was having none of it. In order to avoid those conversations and confrontations, she'd frequented Baker Street less and less, but now that decision was coming back to haunt her as well.

When she'd thought she'd heard Gavan say something about spanking, she'd felt as though her knees might buckle and her pussy might drip with need. Her nipples were in a constant state of arousal around him. The chieftain of Clan Drummond called to the deepest, darkest parts of her body and soul. She wasn't a fool. Not only was Gavan way out of her league in terms of society, but the man was a mafia boss. She'd always felt any woman who got involved with one of those men got what they deserved and the ones who fantasized about them between the covers of a romance novel were fools. Even so, there were times when she'd indulged her need to read a dark mafia novel, imagining herself as the heroine of the story and Gavan as the anti-hero.

It had taken them a while to convince the Fire and Rescue Service their assistance wasn't needed. When the captain in charge of the team started to berate her for calling them if she hadn't wanted them there in the first place, she'd pointed out that it was Gavan Drummond who had sounded the alarm and if there was any penalty to be paid, he ought to be the one to pay it. The captain had backed down so fast, it almost gave her whiplash.

"No. I'm sure Lord Drummond thought he was doing what was best. You might want to thank him for alerting us to ensure your safety and that of your people," the captain had said.

Blaise rolled her eyes. "You can't be serious? He came for a meeting with my grandfather, then stuck his nose in where it wasn't wanted or needed. You want to bow down and kiss his feet? You go right ahead. As far as I'm concerned, the man can kiss my ass."

She walked away, waving the captain off with Tommy on her heels.

"It really doesn't do us any good for you to antagonize Craig. He's just trying to do his job."

Blaise stopped, took a deep breath, and checked her temper. "I know you and Craig are seeing each other and that's fine with me, but the fact is that Drummond isn't the only one who stuck his nose into my business without asking for my permission."

"They only want to help..."

"They only want to help themselves. Look, I get it. They're both control freaks who don't think the wee lassie can run a distillery. Well, they're wrong. I'm going to get Boyd to come out and upgrade our security system and look into hiring a security service to patrol the grounds."

"Geezus, Blaise, you don't think it was an accident, do you?" asked Tommy.

"I wish I did. I checked those stills myself last night. I want to wait until everyone clears out—and I'm only telling you because I trust you—but I want to take a look at Still 1."

"Do you think someone deliberately caused that fire?"

Blaise nodded. "I don't want to, but I'd be willing to bet a lot of money that I'm right."

"Shit! That's it. I'm moving into your guest bedroom and we're calling in the police and an arson investigator."

"Oh for heaven's sake, Tommy, and do what? I'll

have a security patrol and an upgraded system before nightfall."

"And you're out here all by yourself with only Vera and your granddad. Not that I don't think they're lovely people, but Vera's in her seventies and your granddad is dying. Oh shit, Blaise, I'm sorry. That was a hurtful thing to blurt out."

Blaise repressed the tears that wanted so badly to form every time she thought about it. She'd known for some time that her grandfather was dying, but neither he nor Vera seemed inclined to talk to her about it. If him believing that she didn't know was making things easier for either of them, Blaise was willing to play along.

"No, it wasn't."

"You knew?"

"You didn't?" she quipped. "My grandfather is a proud man. He would never have let anyone take care of him if Vera had given him a choice. I think not having to deal with my emotions makes it a bit easier on them both. So, I'll go about my life and when the end comes, I'll deal with it, then I'll miss him for the rest of my life."

"You know you aren't alone. There's not a person who works at Kilted Fire who wouldn't do anything for you or your granddad."

"I know." And she meant those two words.

"I still don't think you ought to be here alone."

"I'll tell you what, if I can't get a security patrol out here tonight, you can stay until I do."

"Do you have any idea who it might be?" Tommy asked.

"Not a freaking clue," she responded.

CHAPTER 5

*G*avan slid his cufflinks in place. He knew French cuffs were considered out of fashion by some, but Gavan didn't care. He liked the way they looked and felt. Besides, he had numerous pairs that had been passed down through the centuries.

There was a soft knock on the door before Hamish stuck his head in. "Gav, Dougal stopped by. He's on the way to Kilted Fire and wanted a moment of your time. He seemed to think it was important."

"I'll be right down. Show Dougal to my study."

Study? It was his office, but study sounded so much more befitting of a seventeenth century castle that had been maintained by the same clan and family who'd built it. Gavan toed his way into the expensive loafers, then joined Hamish and Dougal.

Dougal stood, hat in hand, looking very much like

a man waiting to be led to the gallows. "Dougal? Hamish said you asked to see me." He turned to his second in command. "You can leave us alone." Focusing his attention on Dougal, he continued, "What brings you here?"

The man standing before him had once been one of his own. Two years previously he'd attended a Teine where he'd forced—maybe not forced but coerced—his attentions on one of the tigresses. The girl had repeatedly defended Dougal, saying she was as much at fault as he was, often even demanding that she was equally at fault. While there had been no doubt she'd given her consent and been a willing participant, Gavan had come to the conclusion that she'd been under the influence of alcohol and had been easily talked into it. In Gavan's opinion, which was really the only one that mattered at the end of the day, the girl had been unable to give informed consent.

"I know you banished me, and I'm not saying you shouldn't have, but I had a call from Kilted Fire this morning. Knowing your interest in old Lachlan and his granddaughter, I thought you might like to know."

"I'm listening, go on."

"The call was from Blaise. It seems she wants not only to upgrade their security system but to hire security personnel to patrol the grounds. I know you've had people watching over them for years, so I thought you'd be interested."

"Did she say why?" asked Gavan.

"She didn't say, but there's talk in town that they had a fire up there this morning."

The speed with which information and gossip spread on the island never ceased to amaze him. "Did she indicate that she thought it might not have been an accident?" He'd come to that conclusion when he'd picked up the faint aroma of an accelerant at the distillery on his way out. So, the idea that someone had tried to sabotage Kilted Fire was not much of a shock.

"She was pretty evasive on the subject, but it's the only thing that makes sense. Like I said, I thought you'd want to know." Dougal's posture never relaxed.

"Thank you, Dougal. I know it wasn't easy for you to come here. I appreciate you doing so. Could I ask a favor of you?"

"Of course. Anything."

"Keep me appraised of what you find out, and if you can hire the men I already have in place, I'd be happy to pay for them. That way we won't have people running into one another unexpectedly and you won't have to explain to someone outside the clan what I'm doing there, prowling around conducting my own investigation. My guess is the Fire and Rescue Service will not hear anything about this."

"I wouldn't think so. They say the old man is dying. They're awfully isolated out there."

"An even better reason for my people to be in place. Did she say how many men she wanted?"

"Only two. I tried to tell her she'd need more for the place to be effectively patrolled, but she was adamant."

Gavan smiled ruefully. "She doesn't want the expense. She'd rather risk her own neck than cut back on their production or the quality of their ingredients."

Dougal smiled. "Aye. She's a distiller from the old school, but you must admit she does make one of the best single malts in the world." Gavan nodded in agreement. "I'd be happy to have as many men as you'd let me have and I can afford to pay, especially if I'm charging her. And if I don't charge her, you can bet I'll hear about it."

"I'll pay for them. I don't want the men feeling as if they have any divided loyalties. But you're right, she'll notice if the bill doesn't go up."

"I'll put them on the books and charge her, but then send you a bill for some kind of nebulous service. That way the government doesn't get its nose out of joint and still gets their taxes."

"That will work just fine. I don't know that it'll be for that long. If someone is trying to go after Kilted Fire, I should be able to sort it out fairly quickly. Look, Dougal, I want you to know, I've been watching you since you left the clan."

"Like I said, I wouldn't have come if I didn't think it was important."

"And I appreciate you coming. It had to have been difficult for you."

"That's not true, your lordship. I have never resented or questioned how you handled the situation. I was all kinds of wrong. Debra and I were young and drunk and got carried away, but I should never have done what I did. Even though they weren't seeing each other at the time, I've made amends to her and to her mate."

"They've both gone out of their way to let me know what you've done and to let me know that there are no hard feelings on their side. I know the old ways said no second chances, but maybe we need to take a look at that. I'm not ready to accept you back into the clan, but if you'd like to come to Sunday supper, you'd be welcome, at least on a trial basis."

Poor Dougal looked as though Gavan had granted him the greatest prize.

"I'd be honored, and I know my parents would be grateful."

"You have a lot of people who've been willing to speak on your behalf. I needed to know that your change and remorse were sincere and permanent."

"They are."

"Then we'll see you on Sunday."

As the young man left, Gavan couldn't help but smile. Dougal had done a lot of growing in the past two years. He hadn't once tried to violate his banishment; he'd gone out of his way on more than one occasion for members of the clan. Perhaps it was time for a change.

Blaise tasked her work crew with focusing on Stills 2 through 5 as well as the myriad of other work that went into creating one of the finest single malt scotches in the world. They might not be as big as some or have the money to advertise to increase their customer base, but they had a solid reputation. Her grandfather didn't think she had the ability to run the distillery on her own, but he was wrong.

She had plans to expand, plans to take their whisky into the future. Slowly, but surely, Blaise had been squirreling away money. It had been proof positive to her of her grandfather's deteriorating health that he hadn't noticed. One of her ideas was to approach Gavan Drummond with a business proposition where she would supply their whisky to his exclusive club in Inverness if he would agree that Kilted Fire would be the only single malt served.

With that money, she planned a three-pronged attack: invest in another two kilns, produce a blended scotch, and distribute a twelve year. In the past, Kilted Fire had only produced single-malts and only distributed eighteen year and above whiskys. She'd tried to broach the idea with her grandfather, who'd shut her down without even hearing her out.

For a scotch snob, blended scotches were an abomination. And while she wouldn't drink one, she did see blended and younger, less expensive single-malts as a gateway for those who'd never had a fine scotch to be introduced to Kilted Fire. Blaise believed there was a whole untapped market of younger drinkers who were being lured to what she considered the dark side, which was anything other than an aged, single malt. She had to smile and admit that she was most definitely a scotch snob.

Once the fire was out and the still and coal furnace beneath had cooled sufficiently, Blaise began to poke around the kiln and its heat source. Part of being a great distiller was using all of your senses, including that of touch and smell. Blaise picked up a piece of the cooled coal and brought it to her nose. Sure enough, she could detect the faint aroma of alcohol. Even a layman would think there wasn't much of a surprise there, but Blaise's trained sense of smell told her it wasn't Kilted Fire Alcohol. It wasn't the smooth aroma of a good whisky; this had the jarring notes of pure grain moonshine. She also found a remnant of something that had blocked the ventilation system. Between the two, there was no doubt in her mind that the fire this morning had been arson. *I knew I didn't miss something when I checked the stills last night.*

The question now was what to do with that information. Surely, she couldn't burden her grandfather with that knowledge and despite what Tommy thought, Craig was an idiot. Blaise knew that to keep Craig's nose out of what guessed had happened, she needed to keep Tommy in the dark. Craig and Tommy had been in a relationship for about six months, but she knew both wanted to be further along in their careers before they committed to a future together. Tommy showed promise to move up when her grandfather passed, but he still had a lot to learn, so she wouldn't name him head distiller.

She heard a commotion toward the front of the stillhouse and saw Vera talking to one of the men. After a minute, their conversation ended, and Vera left just before the worker came charging toward Blaise.

"Blaise, it's your granddad. Vera says you need to come."

Ensuring that the still was secure and no one could tell what she was looking at, Blaise stood, wiped her hands, and ran toward the main house.

Finding Tommy she said, "I'm not sure yet what's happening or how long I'll be but keep everyone from Still 1 and keep things moving along."

"Will do. I hope… well, you know," he said sympathetically.

Blaise squeezed his arm. "I know. Thanks."

Briskly, she walked toward the house, steeling

herself for whatever was to come. He'd raised her to be strong and he'd always believed she was far stronger than she was. Now was not the time to disabuse him of that notion. Whatever it took, she would maintain the illusion of strength and a calm demeanor until his time on this earth had passed.

Once inside, she headed to the library that they'd converted to a bedroom when he'd became ill. Blaise had arranged for a new doorway to be installed so that he could access the downstairs bath directly while he was still somewhat ambulatory.

With a deep breath, she opened the door and quietly entered.

CHAPTER 6

*G*avan's mobile rang. What only Hamish knew was that he didn't just have men patrolling the property, he actually had a man inside the distillery.

"Gavan? Vera just came tearing down here and got Blaise. She's gone up to the house now. It doesn't look good."

"I don't want to intrude on their time together or their initial shock and grief at Lachlan's passing. Keep an eye on the situation and keep me appraised," he said, ending the call.

"Trouble?" asked Hamish.

"I think this may be the end for Lachlan. Have you heard anything more about Murdock?"

"Aye. The little weasel is going to attempt to smuggle his drugs through your territory. He knows the Yard knows you don't do drugs and tend to be a bit more lax."

Gavan chucked. "Besides, if he gets caught, he'll try to frame me for it and destroy any good will I have with the Yard."

"Well, you must admit, you gave him cause when you let the cops know when and where his last shipment was coming in."

"I warned Murdock to keep his shit away from my people." Gavan shrugged as if nonplussed. "By the way, I invited Dougal to come to Sunday supper."

Hamish threw himself back in the chair as though he'd been hit. "That's surprising, given that you banished him for violating one of the tigresses."

Hamish could be pretty old school. "He didn't violate Debra. She insisted all along that she'd encouraged him and was a willing participant. Should it have happened? No, but it's not like he forced her. She's spoken to me several times on his behalf."

"I can't see that going over too well with her mate..."

"Actually, Fraser has been quite supportive of Dougal as well. I think the times and attitudes are changing and we're obliged to at least think about changing with them. I'm not ready to rescind his banishment, but I've seen a lot of positive changes in him."

"I can't disagree with that, and I've never once heard him say a word against you, the clan, Debra, or your decision. Still, I worry that'll send the wrong message."

"I'm not sure it doesn't send the right one. Did Dougal fuck up? Damn straight. But so did Debra, and Dougal begged me not to banish her as well."

"I didn't know that."

"At the time, I don't think I gave him credit for that. He wanted her absolved of any wrongdoing and she wasn't having it. They both admitted they didn't have any leanings toward wanting the other to be their mate. God knows Debra's happy with Fraser. If all three of them are willing to let bygones be bygones after Debra and Dougal owned up to their part, let's see how the clan reacts when Dougal comes to supper."

"I know his parents will be thrilled. It's been hard on them."

"I know, but I also know his father was disappointed in the lad. Lad? Good God, he's in his early twenties now. He's long past being a lad. Was Gere able to resolve the situation in Inverness?"

"He was, and I told him there'd be a bonus in his paycheck. That was a heads up move on his part."

Gavan nodded. "It was indeed. I'm not sure I would have noticed there was no duty stamp."

"Me either. It seems our former head bartender at the club was making a little money on the side. We held him out overnight in the warehouse. What do you want to do with him?"

"Do we know how much he took us for?"

"Gere spent all night going through the books and has the figure."

Gavan tapped his chin as if thinking. "Tell our ex-employee that if he pays us what he stole and leaves the UK, I'll let him live."

"I think he'll think that rather magnanimous of you," said Hamish with a smile.

"Haven't you heard? I'm a generous kind of guy."

"Yes, all the subs at the club know you as the cuddly Dom."

Gavan laughed. They didn't and both he and Hamish knew it.

"Do you think Gere is ready to move up?" While Gavan owned the club, Hamish actually ran its day-to-day operations. "I know you've been thinking about making some changes in that area." Gavan trusted Hamish's judgement more than he trusted most people.

"I was. The bar wasn't doing as well as I thought, but I didn't think the guy would actually be stealing from us. I thought about Colleen since she's been with us longer and has a good head on her shoulders, but when I brought it up casually, she nixed the idea. For one thing, she told me she made more money from our members who are good tippers, and for another, she didn't want the responsibility. So, I'd been thinking about Gere."

"I leave that up to you."

"What if the guy won't go or won't pay?"

"Scare the shit out of him, then drop kick his ass to somewhere cold in Canada without a passport. Have our people scrub him from any governmental systems. If we can't get to our money, I'll be damned if he'll be able to get to his."

Hamish laughed. "You do have a wicked sense of justice."

"Did you talk to our guys over at Kilted Fire?"

"I did. They didn't see anything last night. They've done a sweep along the perimeter fencing and haven't found a thing. Why do you ask?"

"I don't think Blaise believes it was an accident and I sure as hell don't. I could detect an accelerant in the air."

"Is that why Dougal stopped by?"

"He wanted me to know Blaise ordered an upgrade in their security system and wants to have actual security guards on site in the evenings. He's going to hire our two guys and I thought we'd assign two more. I want two visible and two not. He'll put the first two on the books and add it to Kilted Fire's bill. He thought I'd want to know."

"How was the old man?"

"Not good. From the look of him, I doubt he'll last much longer." Gavan shifted in his seat uncomfortably.

"Are you ready to take on what he asked?"

"The first one is easy. I actually thought we'd

throw two celebrations, one at Kilted Fire and one a few days later at the club. We can hold it when the club is closed and have it be invitation only. Vera's going to need something to occupy her time and help her through her grief."

"She won't be one to just sit around and weep."

Gavan chuckled. "Hardly. I don't believe she has any family and no real strong ties to Inverness. I thought I might install her at Kilted Fire."

"Won't Blaise have something to say about that?"

"I'm sure she'll have an opinion, but I don't like the idea of the house being empty. Blaise will be here at Cat-Sith."

Hamish raised one eyebrow. "She's not going to give up her home and Kilted Fire just because you say so."

"That's where you're wrong. She will be by my side. I might be willing to allow her to remain as the master distiller at Kilted Fire, but until we find out what's going on, she'll be protected at all times."

"Again, just because you say so?"

"What are you saying?" Gavan asked, his voice beginning to register his annoyance.

"She hasn't been raised as one of our kind and while she might submit sexually, she's not a woman to just give over, let you rule, and meet you at the door, kneeling with your pipe and slippers."

"I don't smoke a pipe."

"Let's just say," Hamish said with a grin, "that it's

going to be really entertaining watching you take your mate in hand."

Hamish left Gavan alone with his thoughts as he looked over the windswept beach. Lachlan's death was going to hit her hard. He wanted to be there for her, to keep her safe, and to make sure she knew she wouldn't be alone; she would be loved and cherished.

Chuckling to himself, he shook his head. That was a lovely dream, and he would make it come true, but he knew it wouldn't be easy. He knew it wouldn't be sweet words and soft caresses that won her over.

She was his mate; she would submit, and he would keep her safe.

As she placed her hand on the door handle, Blaise took a deep breath. Whatever comes, I will survive. She opened the door, and all five senses were assailed. She heard the steady beat of the machines as they monitored his condition and she saw the slow rise and fall of her grandfather's chest as he breathed with only the aid of those same machines. She tasted the bile as it rose from her throat and threatened to spill out. She could feel the specter of death as it closed in on her grandfather.

"He hasn't much time left," whispered Vera. "He wants to talk to you."

She took Vera's hand. "Stay. I know what you

mean to him." Vera nodded and they each took a seat on either side of her grandfather.

The last sense: touch. She held her grandfather's frail hand with its paper-thin skin. That same hand had taught her to drive, to measure and judge the quality of ingredients that went into their fine single-malt whisky, and had dried her tears when her first boyfriend broke her heart. Those hands had always been so strong, so vibrant.

He turned first to his Domme and the woman he'd loved for many years. "I love you."

"I know," Vera said with tears trickling down her cheeks. "There's nothing I need you to say nor anything I need to say to you. You have been the best thing that ever happened to me, and I will love you forever."

"You have given me more peace than I ever dreamed possible. I love you, Ma'am." He turned to Blaise. "And you… you were anything but peace. You were the joy of my life and my shot at redemption for the choice I forced your mother to make. She made the right choice; she chose love."

"Save your strength." said Blaise, trying to hold back the tears.

"I don't have much time left. I need you to know that along with Vera, I have loved you more than any other person in my life. There is nothing that I wouldn't do to see you safe and happy. You have to believe that and trust that I know what I'm doing."

"Granda, save your strength." Blaise looked up at Vera. "Isn't there..."

"Nay, lass. Time has caught me up and I can feel death near. I'm trusting you to take care of my Ma'am. She's like you and thinks she can do it all alone, but neither of you can. Vera and I already arranged the funeral and I asked Gavan to take care of the celebration of life. Let him take the lead and take the weight from your shoulders. Promise me, both of you." The last was gasped as he struggled to breathe.

"We promise," Blaise and Vera vowed in unison.

"You'll have each other, and you'll have Gavan. Trust him. Believe in him. He is the most honorable man I have ever known. I expect to spend a long time in heaven before I see either of you again."

He smiled, taking a deep breath. As the air left his lungs, he was gone. The machines started to sound their alarms and all Blaise could do was hold his hand while Vera stood and turned off the noise around them. She leaned down, stroked his hair away from his face, and kissed his forehead.

"Goodnight, my sweet prince. And may flights of angels sing thee to thy rest." She paused. "I loved him, you know," whispered Vera.

CHAPTER 7

*S*orrow seemed to consume her, not quickly, but bit by bit. They stood in the family cemetery. Normally this was a spot where she found great peace, but today, all she felt was the gnawing grip of pain that had accompanied her grandfather's death and been her constant companion for the past three days. Blaise had insisted that Vera stand with her and had already decided that if she wanted, Vera would be buried in the Munro cemetery on her grandfather's other side. She had to suppress a smile. What would people think hundreds of years from now when there was one man, flanked on either side by women he had loved.

A crowd had gathered for this solemn occasion. She'd expected all of their people to be here, but was surprised and heartened by the number of townsfolk and those from Castle Cat-Sith who'd joined them. They were interspersed among the gravestones and other markers that had been placed here to mark the passing of her ancestors.

On her other side, Gavan Drummond had taken up residence. From the moment Vera had called to let him know of her grandfather's passing, the enigmatic Dom had taken over, bringing in staff to take care of she and Vera. At first, she'd bristled at his interference, but Vera had reminded her that they'd promised her grandfather.

Blaise knew she needed to be here, but her mind was elsewhere. She really needed to stop at the still-house and ensure everything was running smoothly. She trusted Tommy, who, like the rest of the workers, was attending the funeral. Trusting Gavan Drummond, not so much. It wasn't that Drummond had ever done anything to her; there was just something about the man that affected her the same as nails being dragged down a chalkboard. Blaise chalked up the fact that she found him more irritating than usual because of everything else going on in her life.

Her grandfather might be dead, but they had orders to be shipped out and she needed to take a closer look at the books. There were improvements she wanted to make, ones that could open up whole new markets for Kilted Fire. It was up to her, and she meant to make a name for herself as the first woman to run the distillery. Her granda was no longer the face of Kilted Fire as he had been for more than six decades; she was, and she planned to do him proud. Work may have been on her mind, but it was grief that tore through her soul.

The day was bright but cold. They were close enough to the ocean to hear it as it pounded relentlessly against the rocky shore. She pulled her cloak closer, trying to ward off the bitter wind blowing in from the sea. The dress she'd chosen didn't do much to deter the frigid air. The black silk was covered with black silk organza, and it was long-sleeved and V-necked; it hugged her curves and skimmed down past her knees where it ended in a large, loose ruffle.

"Are you warm enough," he whispered as he began to unbutton his cashmere overcoat.

"I'm fine, Gavan. Thank you."

As much as she hated to admit it, she was glad Gavan had been here and glad he'd taken over to ensure things ran smoothly. She found his presence oddly comforting and disturbing in a way she doubted he'd find flattering. She knew the man's reputation as a Dom, and she couldn't judge him for it because they were very alike in many ways. In a deep, dark voice that sounded like hot fudge being poured over ice cream, he'd assured her that he had everything under control, but that if there was something he and Tommy had a question about, he would involve her.

Gavan had suggested, in the way only a Dom could suggest, that she focus her attention on taking care of Vera.

After everyone else had either gone to bed or gone home. Blaise and Vera sat alone in the kitchen, in front of the fire.

"Did you two ever talk about it? Him and me?" asked Vera.

"Not about the nature of your relationship, but he knew that I knew. What he did talk about was how happy you made him. How, until you walked into his life, he'd never thought he'd love anyone again after my grandmother."

"He never talked about her…"

"It wasn't his way," said Blaise. "I think their marriage was arranged. It was as if both sets of parents thought they could take over the other's distillery. In the end, they loved each other, but mostly because my grandmother came to love the land and the whisky we produced. I never met her."

Vera nodded. "He said she died shortly before your parents. He meant what he said. You were the single greatest joy in his life, and he would have done anything for you."

"I know. As hard a man as he could be, he made sure I knew that. Every single day, he made sure I knew how much he loved me and never considered himself to be burdened by having to take in an unruly teenager."

"It doesn't seem to bother you that I was your grandfather's Domme," observed Vera.

"Why should it? You seem kind and it's obvious you two loved each other. I guess I assumed he found the peace and happiness he needed in ceding control and serving you. As I find mine doing the same, I'm hardly in a position to judge."

"But there are a lot of people, even in the lifestyle, who are put off by it."

Blaise squeezed her hand. "Lucky for both of us, I'm not one of them."

The priest finished his committal service and they began to lower her grandfather's body into the ground. She heard Vera catch her breath and linked her arm with the older woman's to hold her close. After the casket was in the ground, she and Vera helped each other to the side of the grave and tossed in a sterling silver rose.

"Goodbye, my darling. You were the best of me. Until we meet again," said Vera, choking back her tears.

"Goodbye, Granda. I'll take care of her and Kilted Fire. You just rest. Thank you for everything. I love you."

Wiping their tears, they turned away from the casket. Her heart ached in an even more profound way than it had when she'd lost her parents. She'd grown into a woman with her grandfather and their relationship had been deep and complex as friends, family, and business partners. She was going to miss him immensely.

Gavan moved to her side and escorted she and Vera down the long path back to the house. He'd arranged not one, but two celebrations of Lachlan's life, one here at the distillery and one at his club in Inverness. The one at the distillery was catered, but he'd still managed to maintain a casual, warm atmosphere.

People gathered at the house where they were ushered in and made to feel welcome. She was glad Drummond had brought some of his own people to help. They weren't in uniforms. That would have given the wake a far too stuffy feeling. Her granda wouldn't have liked that. Drummond's staff had opened up the entire ground floor, and had turned the study from its last purpose as a room for the dying, back into its original use. There were plenty of places for people to sit, mix, and mingle. She could hear people laughing and talking as booze and food began to be consumed. Maybe most would have thought wine more appropriate for a sacred occasion, but her granda had been a whisky maker and so the single-malt and ale flowed.

Even though Gavan had arranged everything, she still moved through the house, talking to different groups of people, allowing people to express their condolences, telling a story or two, and the like. She could see why her grandfather had wanted this and not some maudlin and formal church service. No, this was far more like the man himself—just friends celebrating his life and sharing their memories.

Blaise startled when she felt his hand on her elbow and he leaned down to ask, "When was the last time you ate?"

"I don't know. This morning or last night," she answered, trying to remove her arm from his steely grip.

"Not acceptable. Lachlan tasked me with looking after you. Come with me."

The command note in his voice was clear. The man might be a powerful, dominant, alpha male, but he wasn't her Dom, and he couldn't just give her orders in her own home.

She snatched her arm away from him. "I'm fine, Drummond. I have guests to see to."

"I have ensured your guests will be well cared for. You look as though you're so exhausted that a strong wind could blow you away," he said, taking hold of her again before grabbing a plate with a variety of appetizers and steering her into a small room off the kitchen. "It's not as good as an actual meal, but it'll do for tonight. Starting tomorrow, we'll have breakfast together."

Once inside the room, he turned her loose as he closed the door and she whirled on him. "Starting tomorrow, you can bloody well stay up at your castle and keep your nose out of my business." She knew she was over-reacting, but she didn't care.

"You couldn't be more wrong," he stated calmly, handing her the tray before returning to stand in front of the door. "Sit down and have something to eat."

"I'm not hungry," she lied as her stomach growled.

"I'm not sure who trained you, but Fitzwallace must be losing his touch if a sub from Baker Street thinks she can talk to a Dom in that tone of voice, then outright lie to him. Who trained you?"

"None of your God-damned business."

"What if I'm making it my business?" he asked, closing the distance between them.

"I'll scream."

"You lived here for years and haven't a clue," he said, shaking his head. "Do you know what this room is or its function?"

"It's a kitchen storeroom."

"Yes, specifically, it stored wine and other spirits. When this place was built, whisky and wine were even more valuable commodities than they are now. What that means is that the walls are much thicker and better insulated. So, scream all you like—no one will hear you."

"Look, Drummond. You may be king shit in your club, but this is my home and my distillery, and while I appreciate all you've done in the past few days, it does not mean I'm going to drop to my knees and call you Sir."

"You will only call me Sir in the presence of those outside the lifestyle. In a club or when we're alone, you'll bloody well call me Master."

"You are fucking delusional."

Gavan snorted. "You will also stop swearing. I don't like it."

"Do I sound like a woman who much gives a shit what you like?"

"You sound like an over-tired, over-stressed, and over-worked brat who needs to be taken in hand."

"Never going to happen," she huffed.

"Never say never, Blaise. You won't like having to eat those words."

"It'll be you who does the eating," she retorted.

The predatory smile that spread across his face would have been terrifying if it hadn't seemed to light up all the corners of the room. What might it be like to have this primal male ordering her around, seeing to her needs and pleasure while she saw to his? *Knock that shit off! The last thing I need is Gavan bloody Drummond deciding to take over.*

"Happily and on a regular basis. And if you taste half as good as you smell, I might never get my fill."

Did he just say that to me?

Not able to think of a more mature way to respond, Blaise threw the plate of food at him. She was actually surprised when it hit him because she'd thought he'd move away from the door, or at least duck, but no such luck. The thing hit him squarely in the face. His quick reflexes meant he caught the plate before it could clatter to the floor, bursting into pieces. Slowly, he removed his handkerchief and wiped the food from his face.

"You're going to pay for that."

CHAPTER 8

*B*laise was now faced with a conundrum. He wasn't wrong that she was over-tired and over-stressed, and she'd known for a while that a good session with a Dom who knew what he was doing would be beneficial. But the idea of that Dom being so close to home, and more specifically, being Gavan Drummond, was thrilling and terrifying at the same time. Drummond was an experienced Dom and a man she'd been attracted to for years. He was also, reportedly, the head of the Galloglass Syndicate.

Grabbing her hand, Drummond spun her around and rucked her dress up past her hips before pressing her upper body down onto the harvest table that dominated the center of the room. The fact that this was happening was a source of arousal and surprise. This was a man known for his control in any and all situations. His actions were meticulous and measured.

Could he actually be in control right now? He situated her arms across the small of her back and pinned them there with one hand.

"No panties. Good. You won't need them. You can pick a safeword later. For now we'll use the stoplight system," he growled.

She said nothing. Later, she would question why she'd said nothing. He'd given her a word that would shut everything down—red—and adequate time to say it. The real problem lay in the fact that as he waited, he caressed her exposed backside with a practiced hand before giving each check a firm squeeze. The first swat that landed was firm, but not overly painful, and the next four did nothing but light up her flesh, stiffen her nipples, and cause her to drip with desire for more.

As his fingers slipped between the petals of her sex, she moaned, not in protest, but in need. Dipping them inside, he drew out her silken honey to rub into her swollen clit. He repeated the gesture stroking from clit to slit to dark portal and back again. Instead of thinking about her grandfather's passing and the people gathered outside this room, all Blaise could do was feel. His display of dominance had given her the safe place of her submission.

Drummond smacked her ass harder, the heat blossoming into something far from pleasure as he began spanking her with a strong and steady rhythm, each connection between his hand and her backside seeming to echo in the room. There was pain, but each blow sent tendrils of desire burning through her system, at first like a small, intimate campfire, then like a wild bonfire on a beach.

With every strike, sting, arousal, and anticipation grew exponentially. It had been so long since she'd allowed herself this respite and never had she flown so high. The spanking covered her entire bottom, and she knew there would be evidence of it tomorrow. He spanked the backs of her thighs and under the swell of her ass. Once or twice, part of his hand landed between her legs making her groan and writhe, but not in pain.

Suddenly, he stopped but she could hear him behind her opening his fly and lowering the zipper. He spread her legs, stepping between them as she felt his trousers slide down their thighs. The large head of his cock was poised against her opening.

"Are you with me, Blaise?" The anger from before had been replaced by lust, but the dark voice of the Dom still remained.

"Yes, Sir," she answered without thinking.

Another hard smack to her already aching backside. "What did I tell you to call me when we were alone?"

"No."

His hand descended again, but worse yet, he made no move to breach her with his cock.

"Yes," he growled. "Answer me properly, Blaise, or this will get worse for you."

"How could it be worse? I'm bent over a table with a painful ass, dripping with need and you're just fucking standing there doing nothing about it," she growled. He wasn't the only one who could make alpha noises.

She'd anticipated another blow. Instead, he chuckled. "Aye, well, that's the way between Doms and subs isn't it. Either you answer me properly or it'll be morning before you get my cock. I'll spend the rest of the evening keeping you right on the edge and never giving you what you really want. What do you call me when we are alone, Blaise?"

When she held her tongue, he stepped back, smacked her ass three times and her swollen sex twice, causing her to cry out.

"I like hearing you yowl. Answer me."

Again, she refused to speak and was rewarded with another five swats, even harder than the previous ones. She squirmed and writhed, but he had her trapped and there wasn't anything she could do except give him what he asked for to get what she needed.

"Master."

"Good girl," he purred. "Let's try again. Are you with me, Blaise?"

"Yes, Master." Everything between where his hand held her against the table to where he stood between her splayed thighs burned and throbbed. When he made no move, she relented. "Please, Master."

"Not good enough. Color?"

Knowing he would settle for no less, she gave over. "Green, Master. I'm green."

He slid closer to her sex and barely breached her opening before releasing her hands, grabbing her hips and pulling her backward, impaling her. Blaise cried out as an orgasm washed over her with an intensity and suddenness that took her breath away. Never had she come from simply being mounted. He was larger than she'd expected and the sensation of being so exquisitely full was almost hypnotizing. She felt possessed, her pussy pulsing all around him as he kept still and allowed her to accommodate his size.

"So long," he groaned before tightening his grip and beginning to thrust.

Drummond drew back until he was almost clear of her before driving forward again with a ferocity that startled and enthralled her. Tightening his hold, he began to pound into her. His cock grazed her inner walls, forcing them to accept and surrender to his dominant claiming. Over and over he hammered her pussy as another orgasm crashed around her, devastating her with its strength.

He fucked her with a frenzied need that bordered on primal. She tried to rise up, but Drummond grasped the nape of her neck and pressed down, pinning her in place. Just as she hadn't been able to evade the spanking he'd inflicted on her, she couldn't escape from his mesmerizing control. Pleasure, need, and peace suffused her system as he gave a final brutal thrust, holding himself deep inside as he spilled himself. Her pussy trembled along his length, milking his cock for every last bit of his essence.

Drummond withdrew and she had to stifle a cry from the feeling of loss she experienced. He drew her up from the table and smoothed down her dress.

Clearing his throat, he rumbled. "Now, you behave yourself. We'll get you another plate of food and I'll find a place for you to sit. I expect you to eat."

Blaise was stunned. He'd spanked and fucked her, then expected her to go back amongst a throng of people and eat? All the while as his cum dripped down the inside of her thigh? Was the man insane?

"You drag me in here, toss my dress up over my back, spank my ass, fuck me, then expect me to go back out and make like nothing happened? How fucked up are you, Drummond?"

He smiled, took her chin in his hand, tilted her head back, and lowered his face to hers. His lips hovered against her skin as he whispered, "I can see I did neither action hard enough. I won't make that mistake in the future."

Before she could say another word, he claimed her lips. His tongue invaded her mouth, sweeping through and sliding along hers in a seductive dance. One hand cupped the nape of her neck as the other gripped her wrists, securing them against her back. He took possession of her mouth with the same ruthless dominance he'd used on the rest of her body and with the same mind-blowing results. He kissed her until her knees started to buckle and she was certain she could feel the earth moving beneath her.

The instant she submitted, he relented. "Do you think you can obey me or do you need to have your bottom spanked again? I'll tell you now, you won't get my cock again until I take you to my bed."

Still not willing to give in completely, she looked up at him. "What makes you think I won't walk out there and accuse you of rape?"

"Because we both know that's not what happened, and you have far too much honor to make false accusations. Just so we're clear, you're now my responsibility and will answer to my authority. We can go over the rules later, but for now, do as you're told. No panties and no swearing. Am I clear with my expectations?"

Blaise snorted. "Are you fucking serious?"

The words had barely left her mouth before he'd landed three sharp slaps to her backside.

"I said no swearing, Blaise, and I bloody well meant it. You swear at me when we're alone or in a club, and you'll get spanked then and there. Do it when we're among those who won't understand our relationship..."

"We don't have a fucking relationship..." she started before the spanking he delivered made her dance.

"Do I need to put you over my knee and deliver a more formal discipline session?"

Blaise held her tongue.

"When I ask you a question, I expect an answer." He growled menacingly. She would have taken a step back, but he prevented her from doing so. "And you stay where I put you. Understood?"

As much as she wanted not to comply, Blaise could see no advantage for her in doing so.

"Yes, Sir," she said, deliberately using Sir instead of Master.

Drummond administered three more harsh swats. "Keep it up, brat, and you'll feel my belt across your backside."

"You don't have a belt," she sneered.

"Aye, not tonight, but I rather imagine I can find a good, stout strap. In fact, there's a good leather man in Inverness. Maybe I'll give him a call and have one made to my personal specifications. And I've had my eye on a vintage single tail made out of kangaroo leather that might make a nice addition to my collection."

"You can't be serious."

"Serious as a heart attack. Do you think you can behave?" he asked, arching his eyebrow as if daring her to brat off at him again.

"Yes… Master."

"Better. Let's go get you some more food; you're going to sit down to eat it."

"There are people here…"

"You've lost your grandfather and have been bearing the whole responsibility for the distillery for a while now. People will come to you."

After helping her fix her clothes and hair, he opened the door, taking her by the hand and leading her to the sitting room. He guided her to an empty wingback chair, grabbing another plate of hors d'oeuvres as they passed by tables of food. Not wanting to cause a scene, Blaise could not figure out a way to refuse to sit. When she thought about rising, Drummond placed his hand on her shoulder and pressed down gently.

"Eat, Blaise."

"I told you I'm not hungry."

"You will do as I say. Eat."

"Bastard," she hissed softly, deliberately keeping her eyes straight ahead.

"That's five."

She snapped her head around and stared up at him. "You can't…"

"Can and will," he assured her, which she found annoyingly comforting.

Blaise took a bite of a baked ham and cheese pinwheel. She was sure it was delicious, but it could just as easily have been sheep shit on a cracker. All she seemed to be able to focus on or respond to was the man standing at her side. People came and went, and she barely heard them but somehow managed to mumble replies that satisfied them.

The problem was the longer she sat, the more uncomfortable she became. There were no two ways about it, Gavan Drummond was a Dom who knew how and understood the power of a good spanking. Yes, her ass hurt, and yes, there was a part of her that was mortified that she'd allowed that to happen, but the real problem was that if she was being honest with herself, she felt more centered than she had since her grandfather had fallen ill.

She wasn't aware that Vera had come to sit next to her until the older woman reached across and squeezed her arm. "You look as though you're feeling a wee bit better."

"I think she is. I got her to eat a little," answered Drummond.

"I tried to encourage her, but I wasn't having much luck."

"Not to worry, Vera. You had a lot on your plate. I should have stepped in when Lachlan got sick. At the very least after he spoke with me."

Vera nodded. "Aye, I should have said something."

"You two do know I'm sitting right here, don't you? I don't need either of you looking after me or telling me what to do. Vera, you are welcome to stay in my home for as long as you like. Drummond, I will thank you to leave at the end of the party and never return," said Blaise, her anger on a low simmer.

The fact that Vera looked to Drummond did nothing for her equilibrium, which at best around Drummond was a bit wonky.

"Mind your sharp tongue, Blaise. But she's right, Vera. Lachlan would have wanted you to stay. This house needs someone to live in and take care of it and the garden. I remember you telling me once you loved to garden but that your flat in Inverness didn't give you the space you needed." He glared down at Blaise. "When I'm ready to return to my home, *brèagha*, it will be with you by my side or slung over my shoulder."

CHAPTER 9

*G*avan looked down at her trying to read her
emotions. He knew she was struggling. He
could almost feel the conflict roiling within
her. He'd felt her give over in the storeroom and knew
that she'd found peace in her brief submission to him,
but she hadn't allowed herself that respite for long
and now seemed to be reeling from the idea that she
had done so at all. It was good though that even as
angry and bewildered as she seemed to be, she was
kind to Vera.

Confusion and hurt clouded her eyes. Gavan was
sure she'd expected Vera to come to her aid or at least
to her defense. Blaise had apparently forgotten or
never been taught the primary rule amongst Doms:
never come between a Dom and his or her sub.

He tried to stroke Blaise's hair to offer her some
comfort, but she ducked away. He really did want to

have a word with Fitz about who had trained Blaise. Whoever he was, he had done a lousy job. He'd always known she was an alpha sub, but that didn't bother him. What did was her inability to recognize his authority over her and to see that they belonged together. Once he got her home to Cat-Sith, she wouldn't have much choice.

"I'm not going anywhere with you." As she looked up at him, she was seething, the languid quality that should have still remained from her orgasms and his discipline had left her body completely.

"Aye, you are. Walking or carried, makes no never mind to me," he answered levelly, reminding himself that she was grieving the loss of her grandfather and was completely unaware that her grandfather had asked him to care for her or that she was his fated mate.

Had he claimed her fully in the storeroom, the bonding tether would already be forming. It had taken every ounce of the control he was known for to keep from doing so. The tether would have allowed him to send a resonating sound that only she could hear to help to soothe her, if she'd allow it to. Therein lay what he knew would be a stumbling block for her: would she let him soothe her or would she fight him every step of the way? He really did need to talk to Fitzwallace or whoever knew her best at Baker Street.

"You can't really think you could just sling me over your shoulder and that myself or others wouldn't do anything to stop you, can you? I can assure you that while your status as a mafia thug might work in Inverness, it wouldn't work here."

Gavan chuckled. "First, *brèagha*, I'm no thug. I'm the syndicate kingpin or so Scotland Yard has dubbed me. And second, if you don't believe I hold even more sway here on Skye than I do in Inverness, you haven't been paying attention."

Before she could make another retort, Archibald Campbell joined them. "Dear Blaise, I'm so sorry about your grandfather. Mr. Drummond, it's good to see you. I'm happy you're here to lend a hand to Blaise and Vera."

"I appreciate you coming," said Blaise, pleasantly.

"As you know, I was your father's solicitor both for Kilted Fire as well as his personal holdings. I thought a great deal of him." He nodded toward Vera. "Vera, it's good to see you again."

Vera inclined her head. Interesting. It would appear she didn't think much more of Campbell than he did.

"I don't want to intrude on your grief," continued the solicitor, "but, the four of us should meet in the next few days."

"Why?" asked Blaise suspiciously.

"You are the three principals in Lachlan's will and the law requires that it be read and assets distributed in a timely manner," answered the solicitor.

"My granda included Drummond among the

principal beneficiaries?" asked Blaise. "I expected Vera, but Drummond?" She turned her hostile gaze to him. "What do you know about this?"

The fact was that he was as surprised as she was. Granted, he'd agreed to take Blaise in hand. Well, that wasn't true, he'd promised Lachlan to look after both she and Vera, but Lachlan had known he was a Dom and more than half in love with his grand-daughter. Lachlan had also known that Gavan was a shifter. There could have been no doubt in his mind that Gavan would claim her.

"We may as well get this over with so Mr. Drummond can collect whatever he has coming to him and not be troubled with us. Vera would ten tomorrow morning be convenient for you?" asked Blaise sweetly, completely ignoring the towering alpha.

"If it's convenient for everyone else," replied Vera.

"I can rearrange my schedule to accommodate that," said Gavan.

"Then it's settled," announced Blaise. "Mr. Campbell, can you meet us here in the study at ten?"

"Yes. Thank you for taking care of that so quickly. As I said, I hated to intrude."

"Not at all. We'll see you both at ten tomorrow. Could you do me a favor, Drummond, and see Mr. Campbell out?"

"Keep pushing me, *brèagha*. You'll find out just how far that will get you. Mr. Campbell?" he said showing the solicitor to the door.

"It'll do you no good to antagonize him," said Vera softly.

"I'm not trying to antagonize him, but he seems to think that with granda gone, he's in charge, but he's not."

"Blaise, Gavan Drummond is a Dom. Part and parcel of that, especially for a Dom like Gavan, is taking care of things, of people. He has a deep-seated need to make things easier for you. Just let him do it."

"I don't need him to take care of me or you for that matter. We can take care of each other."

Vera's soft laughter caught her off guard. "I don't think I can provide you with the same things Gavan can, or should I say did?"

Blaise could feel the heat rising in her cheeks. "What are you inferring?" she asked, drawing away.

"I may be an old lady, Blaise, but I'm not dead. Gavan Drummond has made it fairly clear all day to any other man watching that you are off the market and private property. I saw him take you back to the old spirits room off the kitchen with a plate of food. I was glad to see he'd noticed you weren't eating. He picked a place that was private and pretty much soundproof. The food stains on his jacket, coupled with the way you can't seem to find a comfortable way to sit, tells me he's started laying down the law."

Blaise was thankfully saved from responding in the

heat of the moment by another person giving her their condolences. As she and Vera talked, people came and went, offering their sympathies and their goodbyes as the celebration began to wind down. Blaise kept a sharp eye out for Drummond, who seemed to have left, something she was grateful for.

Sitting back as the last dwindlers filed out, Blaise said, "In case you didn't notice, I'm not wearing his or anyone else's collar and Gavan Drummond is not my Dom. I understand you and my grandfather were exclusive and had a deep commitment to each other, but I just like to play and do scenes in a controlled environment. Drummond was worried I wasn't eating. I thought he was being an interfering old busybody and told him so. I threw the food at him, which was childish, so as a peace offering, I agreed to munch on some of the appetizers. Nothing more, nothing less. The sooner he's gone, the better I'll like it."

"Hmm," said Vera as if she were pondering something. "Did your grandfather ever tell you what I did for a living?"

"I believe he said you were a landscape designer."

Vera nodded. "For the past decade, yes. But before that, I was with Scotland Yard. I was a damn good cop, which means it takes a lot to pull the wool over my eyes. You're right about your grandfather and me. We loved each other very much, and we buried him this morning with my collar. It's difficult for some men to wear one, so his was a bracelet I had made for him.

I buried it with him and will never have another sub. Oh I might play occasionally if someone needs an old lady Domme, but I won't ever experience that kind of love and connection with another."

Blaise could feel Vera's grief. She knew that she'd loved her granda, but the pain in Vera's voice and on her face was palpable.

"He loved you, too. Regardless of what the will says, I meant it when I said you're welcome to stay for as long as you like. It's a big old house and those flower gardens could use a lot of T-L-C so I hope you'll consider it."

"And Gavan?"

"Can go to hell for all I care. Seriously Vera, how can you, a retired police officer, frequent a club owned by a mobster?"

Vera laughed. It was the first time she'd heard her do so with such abandon in a long time. "The Gallo-glass Syndicate is a unique beast to Scotland. It has counterparts in England, Wales, and Ireland. The organized crime unit doesn't understand completely how they work, but we do know they operate differently and outside of most organized crime families. None of them will touch drugs. They have odd rules about prostitution and protection. They don't kill unless necessary and it needs doing. Most of their money seems to come from smuggling and arms dealing, but never with those seeking to harm the UK or our allies. And they seem to exhibit a great deal of control and constraint over other syndicates and cartels. Those who live in their territories are incredibly protective including the local constabulary."

"You almost sound like you like and admire him."

"I do. I like Termonn. I like the people who frequent it and play there. When people walk through the doors, they can shed the skins they show to the outside world and be themselves. I've spent many a fun evening talking to Gavan. He's well liked and there isn't a straight female sub in the place who wouldn't like to spend more time with him, especially if it involved more than bondage suspension, impact play, or discipline. He's a strange man. The rumor is he hasn't fucked a woman in years. He plays, he gets blow or hand jobs, but hasn't sunk himself into a woman in a long time."

Blaise wondered if that was true and why he'd chosen to break his fast in such a spectacular fashion with her.

Vera continued, "You may not believe you have a connection to Gavan Drummond, but he does, and people will be more inclined to listen to him than to you. Even if not for the long term, Blaise, what could it hurt to let him take a little of the burden off your shoulders? Maybe even give you a little bit of pleasure and fun?"

"Thanks, but I get what I need at Baker Street."

Vera looked as if she were about to say something

but thought better of it. Blaise noticed the hour had grown late and Drummond still seemed to be absent.

"The hour is late, and I don't know about you, but I'm knackered. I want to go check the stills," said Blaise.

"Tommy said he'd do it."

"I'm not comfortable having anyone else do it right now. You go on up to bed. I'll turn the security system on, check things over, then turn in myself."

"Did you get enough to eat? I can make something."

"You make whatever you like for yourself. I just want to check on a couple of things, then I'll be in bed."

Vera reached for her arm. "Blaise, what's bothering you? It isn't just your granda. Are you worried about the reading of the will tomorrow? I didn't expect anything and don't need it. I'll happily turn it over to you."

Blaise laid her hand over Vera's. "You're family, Vera. Whatever he wanted you to have, I want you to have. Everything is fine. I just need a few minutes to myself." As she slipped out the back door, she could feel Vera's eyes following her.

There was no way for Blaise to know that it wasn't only Vera who watched.

CHAPTER 10

She watched as the last of the cars of those attending her grandfather's celebration of life pulled out of the drive and onto the coastal highway. She headed first into the malting barns where the harvested barley was steeped in water before being laid out to germinate on the malting floors. From the malting barns she headed to the kiln houses to check on the drying process. Kilted Fire had been set up so that each process resided in a different building to ensure there was no cross contamination. Workers generally stayed in their own area, but each time they left or entered a building they were required to wash their hands and boots.

After checking the other buildings, she entered the stillhouse. Once again, as she had every night since her grandfather had gotten sick, she checked each individual still. All were working properly and had been prepared for the night. Tommy had done his job, as she'd expected he would. Assured that everything was as it should be, she headed up the path to the family graveyard. She wanted a chance to say a private goodbye to her granda.

"It was a great party," she said, kneeling in the damp earth at his grave site. "I made sure Vera knew she was welcome to stay for as long as she likes. Gavan Drummond suggested she might want to take on the flower gardens. I know you always wanted me to do that, but we both know I can grow barley with the best of them, but I have a black thumb where flowers are concerned."

Lost in her own thoughts, she sat still for a moment.

"What were you thinking bringing a man like Gavan Drummond into our lives? I know you played at his club, but seriously Granda, a mafia boss? What the hell did he do that you included him in your will? I don't understand and now I'm talking to a corpse." She shook her head. "I suppose there's nothing to do for it until Campbell tells us what's what in the morning."

When Blaise rolled up onto her feet, she caught movement in the darkness out of the corner of her eye.

"Hello?" she called. "Is there anyone there? Show yourself."

She stood poised for fight or flight, but nothing

answered her, nor did anything else move. After a few minutes where she was absolutely still except for breathing, she turned back toward the house, vowing not to leave it again after dark without a shotgun. She still wasn't convinced that the fire hadn't been set deliberately.

With her granda dead, Kilted Fire could be in trouble. He'd always kept the books himself, so she had no idea where they stood financially. Could her grandfather have owed Drummond money? Was he being given something out of the estate to settle a debt?

God, why did all thoughts lead back to Drummond? She felt a shiver pass through her body at the thought of the man. How could she have let him spank her, much less fuck her? She breathed in, smiling. At least she could be honest with herself. It had been a glorious fuck, probably the best she'd ever or would ever have. Why the hell did he have to be someone she wanted nothing to do with?

As she walked, a thought occurred to her, if Drummond had wanted her bad enough to fuck her the way he had, maybe they could work something out. Inverness was a hell of a lot closer than London. With her grandfather dead, there wouldn't be any more weirdness at his club. Maybe they could outline a D/s contract to play and scene together. She could have him take care of her needs that way. She could limit the scope of their play and write into the contract that it was for the club only and that he was to keep his distance from her outside of that location.

Feeling comfortable with her decision, Blaise entered the house and set the alarm before heading up to her bedroom. She stripped out of the dress and hung it on a hanger. She might need to take it to the secondhand shop. She wasn't sure she'd ever want to wear it again. Under the hot shower spray, the water seemed to reignite her need. She turned it to cold and washed quickly, then dried herself thoroughly before crawling into bed naked and pulling the covers over her body.

The following morning dawned bright and clear. She could tell the sea was up when she opened her windows. The tang in the air was more present as was the sound of the ocean. She decided that at least for a while she would wear black. Accordingly, she pulled on black jeans, tucked into black riding boots, plus a V-neck, cable-knit sweater. She took care with her make-up and instead of a high ponytail, she did a quick, loose French braid. The result was a polished, casual look. As she tied off the braid, she wondered if Drummond liked pulling a woman's hair during sex.

She joined Vera in the kitchen for breakfast before running out to check in with Tommy and the rest of their workers. As she headed first to the stillhouse, she noticed Drummond's Range Rover parked in front. She kept herself busy giving orders and making sure they were running on schedule.

"You could take some time off, Blaise," said Tommy.

"Actually, it feels better to be busy. We have to meet with the solicitor this morning to go over granda's will..."

"We?"

"Yeah. Me, Vera, and Gavan Drummond."

"Gavan Drummond, the mafia boss?" Tommy squeaked.

"One and the same. I take it you don't know why my grandfather would have named him in his will?"

"Haven't a clue. Hell, I didn't even know they knew each other."

That was odd. She would have thought that if nothing else, Tommy would know that her grandfather had been a member of Drummond's club, but why should he? After all, just because he was gay didn't mean he was into kink. And if he wasn't into kink, he might not even know about Drummond's club. She often forgot that those not into the lifestyle were often clueless about such things.

She re-entered the house via the same door, stopping in the kitchen to grab a bottle of water before heading into her grandfather's—now her—study. It was large room with a decidedly masculine flair. The cleaners Drummond had sent had done an outstanding job; there was no trace left behind of the hospice room it had become in the last weeks of her grandfather's life. Once again it smelled of leather, wood, and fine cigars.

There were large bookcases along one wall filled with first editions. The wall opposite was a window wall that had wooden storage files beneath it with a cushioned window seat. Flanking the windows were more bookcases with more first editions. The other two walls were wainscoted with dark green walls above.

In her mind's eye, she saw one wall with Georgian floral print wallpaper, and the other painted a coordinating color with old pictures and diagrams she'd found from when Kilted Fire had been established. She didn't want to erase the presence of all those who had gone before, but if this was to be her study, she wanted to leave her own mark on it.

She entered to find, as expected, that Drummond was already here, and Vera had brought in coffee. There was also a tray of pastries, some of which looked savory, but what really caught her eye was the large, gooey cinnamon roll with a huge glob of cream cheese frosting.

"Look what Gavan brought us," said Vera gaily.

"I didn't know Martin's opened this early."

Martin's was the local bakery, reputed to have been funded, as were several other businesses, by Drummond.

"It doesn't..." he started to reply.

"Unless you're a mafia boss and you make him an

offer he can't refuse?" Again with the tugging of the tiger's tail, she thought.

"Not at all. My cook is his sister and has the same family recipes. I had them brought over this morning."

"Brought over? What, did you go to your club after you left here?" She hoped the pang of jealousy she was feeling wasn't coming out in her voice.

"Jealous, *brèagha*? You have no need to be. No. I told you when I left here, I'd have you with me. Would you like to come to the club? I know you thought about joining at one point."

"The idea of seeing my grandfather in a kink club kind of creeped me out. Sorry, Vera, no offense intended. And by the way, Drummond, you're full of shit."

"That's ten," he said calmly.

She glanced in his direction, careful not to look him in the eye. Instead, she looked past him to the clear sky outside the windows across the room.

"None taken, sweetheart. He felt the same way and was glad when you didn't join. But you might reconsider. It's just a little over two hours from here, a lot closer than Baker Street in London."

"Anyone know where Campbell is?" Blaise said with irritation. "He's the one who called this meeting. He could at least be on time."

Gavan glanced down at his watch. "He's still got a

few minutes, Blaise. Settle down." The last was said with a darker note to his voice.

"I have things to do, and daylight waits for nobody."

"I think I hear someone coming up the drive," said Vera. "I'll go let him in."

As she left them, Drummond chuckled. "Don't expect Vera to stay between us forever."

"I don't need Vera's protection. Need I remind you that I have no collar, no contract, nor is there any kind of understanding between us, and even if there was, none of it is legally binding. You can't actually own anyone. You do know that, right?"

"There is an understanding between us, and I do own you. As for the contract, we can have one if you like and you have both a collar and a ring. I just haven't bestowed them on you… yet."

"Bestowed?" Blaise rolled her eyes. "You're an arrogant jerk, I'll give you that."

"You'll give me a whole lot more than that."

"If you weren't at your club or your castle, where were you?"

"I stayed here last night. I wanted to be close in case you or Vera needed me."

Before she could respond, Vera returned with the solicitor.

Glancing at her watch, Blaise said testily, "You're late. Let's get this over with."

"Let the poor man get a cup of tea or coffee. Just

because you're angry with me is no reason to snarl at anyone else. Take a minute Campbell. Get yourself something to drink. There's also some pastries."

Blaise stood, slapping her hands on the desk, and leaning forward. "Last time I checked, Drummond, this was still *my* house, and he was *my* grandfather."

He didn't rise, didn't even come forward in his seat. "And I told you to stop testing me, *brèagha*. You won't like how I respond. Sit down and behave yourself."

"Quit calling me pretty. I don't like it."

"But you are pretty."

"I am not, and it doesn't matter." Blaise turned her wrath on the solicitor. "Well? Get your refreshments, then get on with it."

"Blaise," said Vera calmly. "Would you like Mr. Campbell and I to give you and Gavan the room or would you like to behave in the polite way I know you were raised and allow the poor man to take a moment before he reads your grandfather's will?"

How dare she turn on me? I guess Doms feel they have to stick together.

"Fine," Blaise said, flopping down in the desk chair. "Since none of you seem to be concerned with my schedule, you've got until ten thirty to tell me what the fuck is going on, then I'm going to work, and you can do whatever the hell you want."

She knew she was being unfair, bordering on

outrageously rude, but she really had all she was going to tolerate.

Gavan turned to Vera. "Perhaps you and Mr. Campbell might adjourn to the sitting room. Blaise is in need of my undivided attention. And that makes fifteen."

Blaise leaped to her feet and then gathered herself. The last thing she needed was to be alone with Drummond. "Vera is right, Mr. Campbell. I was raised to be a more gracious hostess. Please make yourself comfortable. If we could get this concluded as quickly as possible, I'd really appreciate it."

"Certainly, Ms. Munro, and I do apologize for being tardy."

Gavan chuckled. "Nice save, Blaise, but you still owe me fifteen."

After eating two of the pastries and drinking a cup of tea, Campbell shuffled his papers into some semblance of order. "Then let's begin. We can do this one of two ways, either have a formal reading where I read the legal document all the way through, then we discuss anything you have questions about, or I can simply read the bequests and terms, giving you a copy of the document to read at your leisure. Again, if there are questions, I'm here to answer them. My goal is to make this as easy as possible."

"I would prefer to do it the easier way. Vera? Drummond? Do either of you have an opinion?"

Vera was so calm as she said, "Simpler is always better, I think. Gavan?"

"Whatever is easier for the two of you is fine with me. I guess that means we go with short and sweet."

The solicitor adjusted his glasses. "Then this should be, I would think, relatively quick as Mr. Munro's will is fairly straightforward." He cleared his throat. "To Vera McDonald, who brought me a serenity and one of the two greatest joys I've ever known, I leave the caretaker's cottage and two acres of land, should she want them. If not, they will revert to my estate. In addition, the sum of one million pounds to do with as she sees fit."

"Oh, my lord. Blaise, it's too much. Of course, you can have the cottage and the land and I'll let you decide on the money."

Blaise smiled. "I'll take the cottage and land back only if you agree to live on in the house and take over looking after the flowers. As for the money, if he left you a million, he knew what he was doing."

Vera reached across the desk and squeezed her hand. "Of course, I'll stay."

"To my darling granddaughter, Blaise Munro, who was my other great joy but not as much serenity, I leave the house and the immediate five acres plus a forty-nine percent interest in the Kilted Fire distillery..."

"What?" said Blaise, blinking back tears. "Forty-nine percent? He left me forty-nine percent. How much cash?" she said trying to calculate quickly what it would take to buy, if not the other fifty-one percent, at least two percent to give her a controlling interest in the business.

"I'm afraid with the expenditure of the one million to Ms. McDonald there isn't a lot of liquid cash."

"As I said, I'll give you the money, Blaise. This is your home, and you are the rightful heir to the distillery." She turned to the solicitor. "When was this will made? Perhaps we can argue diminished capacity."

"I'm afraid not. The will is very clear that if anyone contests the conditions, they will be excluded, and their share distributed in the same percentages as the remainder of the bequests. There is also a clause that says ownership of the company cannot be transferred from the two recipients, for the period of one year from the date of the reading of this will, or the distillery will be closed, its assets sold, and the proceeds distributed to various charities."

"Then who got fifty-one percent of my…" Blaise's eyes widened in horror. "Oh no, he didn't. He couldn't have." She stood so forcefully that the chair hit the back wall. She whirled to glare at Drummond. "You! It's you. Isn't it?"

CHAPTER 11

*T*his was a royal clusterfuck. That wily old man hadn't left anything to chance. Gavan could have handled Blaise. The way she'd surrendered to his dominance had proved that, but Lachlan had hedged his bets. He'd given Blaise no way out. If he'd thought that might make Blaise more malleable, he hadn't known his granddaughter at all.

"Calm down, Blaise," said Gavan.

"Don't tell me what to do, you bastard," she snarled.

"Twenty," he replied, looking at her levelly. "Now, sit down." He waited for her to reluctantly retake her seat. "Go ahead, Mr. Campbell."

"Perhaps we should wait. Ms. Munro seems to be in great distress…"

"Trust me, time is not going to fix that situation. Please proceed so we know what we're dealing with and can make plans accordingly. I suggest you do this as quickly as possible."

"Yes, Sir. He also left Ms. Munro fifty-one percent of the liquid cash. As for the rest of Kilted Fire, fifty-one percent is to be given to you, Lord Drummond, as well as forty-nine percent of the liquid cash."

Gavan chuckled. "He really did want us joined at the hip."

"What's his share of my company worth?" Blaise asked.

"You'd have to have an evaluation done, but I would millions. Your share of the cash wouldn't purchase it." Campbell answered the unasked question.

"Fine. I don't need all of it. I need you to have an evaluation done. I'll buy two percent to get the controlling interest in my distillery from Drummond," Blaise said.

"Don't bother, Campbell. Apparently, Blaise has forgotten that little clause that states there will be no transferring of ownership for one year from today. Besides, I have no intention of parting with my majority share. No amount of money will ever buy any portion of my fifty-one percent of the distillery. As much as your grandfather wanted us together, I want it even more. Face it, Munro. You're stuck with me."

A frightening calm had taken over Blaise. She pushed back from the desk, stood, and walked to the sideboard. Without a word, she picked up a heavy cut-crystal tumbler, poured two fingers of what he assumed was Kilted Fire scotch, and threw it back, swallowing it in one gulp as if it were water.

Drawing a deep breath, she said, "As I said, I have a busy day. Thank you for coming, Mr. Campbell. Vera, could you show him out? I need to get down to the stillhouse."

"Hold up, Blaise," growled Gavan. "Vera, if you could show Mr. Campbell out and give Blaise and I some time alone, I'd appreciate it."

"Good enough, Gavan, but if you break her heart, I'll use my million dollars and hire an assassin to take you out," Vera said, seriously.

Again, Gavan chuckled. "I'll give you a list of names of guys who'll do it for free."

Vera smiled. "You're a rascal, Gavan Drummond. I'll see the two of you have the house to yourself."

Vera stood and escorted a gobsmacked Campbell out to his car.

As the door closed behind them, Gavan joined her at the side table. "Can I pour you another? I think I'll have one as well." Not waiting for her to answer, he poured her another single shot as well as a double for himself. She arched her eyebrow at him. "You're two ahead of me; I'm just trying to catch up." They clinked glasses and downed the dark honey-colored liquor. "Smooth. Why is it I could never get your grandfather to supply the club?

He'd let me buy enough for myself but not for the club."

"Maybe he didn't like you. I know I don't."

"That's not true and we both know it, but I'll let you have that little falsehood for now. So, what are we up to? Twenty?"

She slammed the glass down on the sideboard. "You can't be serious! You just stole half of my distillery, and you want to spank me for my fucking language?"

"That makes twenty-five, and I want to spank you for a myriad of reasons, chief among them is it got us both incredibly aroused. I will spank you for swearing as I told you that you weren't to do it, yet it would seem you need a lesson in the consequences of disobeying me."

She shook her head. "I was right. You truly are delusional." She walked back over to the desk and picked up a copy of the will. "I'll hire my own solicitor and have him or her go over this thing with a fine-tooth comb. If I can't break it, then I'll have an evaluation done and purchase at least controlling interest in the business."

"I told you. I won't sell. And the will specifically prohibits any transfer of ownership for a year. Besides, I have a hell of a lot more money and influence than you do. You'll never win in a court of law."

"Are you planning to sell your share to anyone else?"

"No."

"I won't be your money cleaner," she said.

His brow wrinkled in confusion until he realized what she meant. "You mean you won't let me launder money through Kilted Fire."

"Whatever. I won't be a part of your illegal and ill-gotten gains."

"You do know when your peat fields ran out and the one time your barley crop failed, your grandfather smuggled what he needed onto the island. Also, for the most part, laundering is only needed for illegal gambling and drug money. I have enough legit businesses of my own to take care of the first and I don't touch drugs. Not now, not ever."

"What are you going to do then?"

"I thought I'd do what I've done with other businesses I either acquire or invest in: let you run it and take my share of the profits. I want to see a detailed business plan by the end of next week and you're going to hire more people to help in the office, plus at least one staff person for the house."

"It's my house."

"They're my rules."

"What else?"

"No swearing, no panties, stay where I tell you, and until we know for sure that fire wasn't arson, no leaving the house, the castle, or anywhere I take you after dark without my express permission."

"That's ridiculous. There are things I need to do."

"Do them before sunset or after sunrise. I mean it, Blaise. I will keep you safe and neither of us is convinced that fire was an accident."

"I never said that to you." Her spine was board stiff at this point in their conversation.

"You didn't have to. I took a closer look at the coal. It was doused with an accelerant, and it looked like someone tampered with the ventilation system."

"Or maybe you did it, trying to get control of Kilted Fire? When did my grandfather make out his new will?"

"Before he talked to me, and he talked to me after the fire. Right now, the only two people who aren't on my suspect list are you and Vera."

"You can't suspect everyone else," she said disdainfully.

"I can and do. Guilty until proven innocent."

"You're paranoid."

"I'm cautious. A man in my position has to be."

"I'm not part of the deal, Drummond."

"That's where you're wrong. You are the deal, Blaise."

"This is a pointless conversation. I need to get to work."

"Pointless or not, it's a conversation we're going to have. I'm going to do what your grandfather asked me to do and you're going to fall into line."

"Why would I do that?" she asked angrily. "Seriously, Drummond, what's in it for me?"

"Fifty-one percent of the business and forty-nine percent of the cash. That's a hell of a lot."

"Is it? And is it if I have to give up what's most important to me to get it?"

"What's your other option? Walk away with nothing? Walk away from your family's heritage and legacy?"

"Maybe."

Watching her world spin out of control was almost more than Gavan could stand. Lachlan had understood far better than Gavan had thought the feelings Gavan held for his granddaughter. She felt trapped and betrayed; but he knew he had to give her a way out, something that would give her a better reason to stay than to go.

"That would be a stupid thing to do, and you have never been stupid. Let's both admit that your grandfather put you in a difficult position..."

"Not difficult, impossible."

Gavan shook his head. "No, difficult. He managed to hitch us both to the same plow. Give him credit; it was pretty crafty on his part. Frankly, I would have bet he wasn't capable of that level of deviousness."

"What's your point, Drummond?"

"My point is that he has us trapped. You can walk away, but that wouldn't be in your best interest or that of the company or its workers. I could walk away..."

"But you won't."

"No, I won't. I'd be walking away from a small

fortune. But what if I make it worth your while to work out a new deal with me."

"I'm not interested in making a deal with you."

"I don't believe that. I think you'd like nothing more than to have someone show you a way you can come out of this with what you want." His voice was calm, cool, and collected as usual.

"You don't even know what I want," she said as the high degree of anger that had fueled her to this point started to wane.

"You're wrong. I think I know far better than you'd like me to what you want and need. Aren't you even interested in what I have in mind?"

She sighed. "I'm listening."

"Let's agree we both want to see Kilted Fire and its employees survive and thrive." She nodded. "Good. Let's also agree that if we fight or try to change the conditions of his will it's going to cost both of us more than we want to give."

"Are you going to get to the point any time soon?"

"My point, *brèagha*, is that it's in both of our best interests to find a way to work together." He held up his hand to keep her from arguing. "So, let's you and I strike a deal. We'll make a secret pact just between the two of us. We'll abide by the terms of your grandfather's will and at the end of the year, I'll sell you my fifty-one percent of Kilted Fire."

"At what price?"

"A single pound."

"Pound of what? Flesh?" she asked suspiciously.

"No, I'll sell my share of the company to you for one-pound sterling. But I do want my pound of flesh, so the deal is that I'll sell you my share of Kilted Fire provided you agree to be my sub for the next year."

"What? Are you kidding me?" she asked outraged.

Gavan shook his head. "Not at all. After last night, I am chiding myself for having avoided making a claim for you in the past. So, for one year as my sub and a single pound, Kilted Fire is all yours."

"Agreed."

The way she so quickly acquiesced made him want to seal the deal by stripping her naked, laying her out on the desk and having at her like a starving man at a banquet.

"Before you agree, hear me out. We will sign a D/s contract, spelling everything out including the terms of your acquisition of my fifty-one percent. For the duration of the contract, you will wear my collar and abide by my rules."

"What about sex?"

"I won't lie to you, I'm going to do my damndest to seduce you and get you to agree to have sex with me, but when we write the contract, everything will be mutually agreed upon. However, for the duration of the contract, you will not play, scene, or have sex with anyone but me."

"You won't try to fuck me?"

Gavan chuckled. "I won't force the issue, but I

warn you, I can be very persuasive. I will, however, require that you act as my sub at home and at the club, which means you will agree to play and scene with me. Agreed?"

"Not so fast. I'm not agreeing to scene with you."

"Not negotiable. You can make a determination about sex, and I will honor your safeword, but scening and exclusivity are non-negotiable."

She paused before saying her next words. "On both sides."

"For me, after I sank my cock into your sweet pussy last night, that was a given. Are we agreed?"

"Do I have a choice?" she asked, anger creeping into her tone.

"Not really. You owe me twenty over my knee. We may as well get it over with."

"I am not going to—you can't really expect me to..."

"I can and I do."

Gavan sat down and patted his thigh. "Now, Blaise."

He tried to disguise the deep breath he took as he reminded himself she was going to require patience as well as discipline. She had no idea, but her entire life had just taken a massive turn.

"I can't—I won't..." she stammered.

Gavan observed her face and body language. She wasn't afraid. She was... embarrassed? What could she be embarrassed about? It wasn't as if she'd never been disciplined; it wasn't even as if he'd never disciplined her. Going on a hunch, he subtly scented the air and had to suppress a grin as his cock tightened behind his trousers. Blaise was aroused and didn't want him to know.

"You can and you will. You're going to submit to my authority because I require it. It is, after all, how Doms communicate their displeasure with their subs and allow them to atone. Make no mistake, Blaise, you are mine. Even if your grandfather hadn't left me a damn thing in his will, I would have claimed you. He gave me his blessing the day I met with him. That's what he wanted me to do."

He watched her emotions play across her face. Confusion, anger, hurt, grief: they were all there and she was entitled to each and every one of them. She wasn't ready to hear she was his fated mate, not ready to learn who he truly was. She thought his being the leader of a syndicate was the thing that separated them, but it wasn't. It was the truth of who, and what, he truly was that could be their undoing.

"If I submit to your rules..."

"And accept my authority."

Blaise nodded. "And accept your authority, you'll let me run the distillery with no interference and sell me your share at the end of the contract."

"Yes. I will let you run the day-to-day operations of the business, but we'll have regularly scheduled meetings each week. If you break any of the rules, you'll also accept my discipline."

"You and my grandfather have really not given me much of a choice. Between the two of you, it's a toss-up as to who I despise more in this moment."

"Careful, *brèagha*. If we're agreed, then we will start with twenty over my knee. Right here. Right now. Strip those jeans off and put yourself here." He motioned to his lap. "And I hope for your sake you aren't wearing panties."

"I'm not. I..."

"Blaise, you will push those jeans off that gorgeous ass of yours and put yourself over my knee. If I have to come get you, it'll be another ten."

She walked over to him and stood between his knees. He'd had plenty of women in that same position over the years, but none had called to him the way she did. But then none had been his fated mate. When her hands went to her button, then to the zipper of her jeans, opening the fly so she could shimmy out of them, his cock began to throb.

Patience, he reminded himself. *Patience*.

Pussy, his cock screamed. *Pussy!*

CHAPTER 12

*A*s her jeans skimmed down over her backside that was still a bit tender from the night before, she questioned her own sanity. Was she really going to do this? Was she really going to let Gavan Drummond spank her? Worse yet, was she really going to let him collar her and accept him for her Dom? Who was she kidding, the idea of spending a year with Drummond as her Dom had all kinds of possibilities. After all, the next year was going to be incredibly stressful, and she could probably use the structure and support he could provide. Besides, regardless of the fact that he was a gangster, he was an incredibly successful businessman and might be able to teach her a thing or two.

"What's your safeword?"

"Bourbon to stop. Gin for a breather. Tequila for good to go."

He chuckled. "Good enough, and we're clear on what we're both agreeing to?"

"Yes. You want me to be your sub for a year in exchange for selling me your share of the distillery for a pound at the end of that time."

"And you're clear on what I expect in a sub?"

"I guess," she said, confused.

"Let me be clear. With the exception that whether we have sex is yet to be determined, you will be my sub twenty-four-seven. You will allow me to act as your Dom in all circumstances, business and otherwise. I will be responsible for you and ensure that you are safe and that your needs are provided for."

"I run the distillery."

"To a certain extent. We will act as partners. You're smart enough to know there are ways to improve the business. I will act as your mentor as well as your Dom."

She nodded and placed herself over Drummond's hard thigh. The cool air wafted across her exposed backside. Time crawled by as she heard the mantle clock slowly ticking away. She couldn't understand why she was so nervous. It wasn't like he hadn't seen it. Hell, he'd had his dick shoved up her pussy last night. That same hard cock was now pressed against her, throbbing.

Drummond's left hand rested on the small of her back as his right one caressed her naked skin. He allowed his fingers to explore the exposed skin in a way he hadn't the previous night. He squeezed each cheek gently and her anticipation for what was going to happen heightened in a way it never had before.

His right hand broke the connection and created a swift uptake of air before it came crashing back down. Connecting in a harsh strike, a flash of pain morphed into a rush of arousal that sizzled along every nerve. *God, he had a wicked hand.* But as it always did, the pain promised the peace of release. Before last night, it had been far too long since she allowed herself to check out mentally, let the world drift away and find peace.

Blaise braced her hands against the floor for balance. "I've got you, *brèagha*. You'll take my discipline, but I'll give you so much more."

"Yes, Master."

"Good girl," he said as he began spanking her with a strong, steady rhythm.

He wasn't asking her to count, which she appreciated, but she trusted him to give her exactly what he promised. Why was it she trusted him? He was a gangster for God's sake. She didn't know the answer; she just knew it was true. She knew he could provide her with what she needed. Was it possible she could do the same for him?

As he continued to rain his discipline down on her ass, she moved her hands from the floor to grasp his leg. It gave her just as much balance, but it felt like a more personal connection. In the past, if she was receiving a spanking bent over a man's knee, it had been more of an exchange of services, but this was different, and God help her, she wanted it.

The spark of desire that had ignited when his hand first smacked her ass had accelerated into a blaze that was burning throughout her system. Heat and pain danced together in a flame that lit up her body and soul. Drummond hadn't been joking when he'd called it discipline. This was no erotic or playful spanking. It seemed he meant to cure her of her cursing. She smiled as the thought that her grandfather would have appreciated that briefly floated through her mind.

Tears welled as her thoughts found that blessed neutral gear and she just…drifted. Here there was no sorrow, no grief, no responsibility. Here she existed out of time and space. For her, there was pain, but there was also peace and arousal. Gavan Drummond, however, didn't need to spank her to get her aroused. No, all he had to do was be.

As she let go and let the tears fall, she realized what a release it was after the last few weeks of her granda's illness and passing. She could feel them beginning to cleanse and restore her soul. She would always miss him, always be grateful for everything he'd done for her, and maybe even be grateful for having forced her into Drummond's sphere of influence.

At the end of what she was sure was twenty swats,

his hand descended and began to caress the heated flesh.

"You took that well, *brèagha*. You're gorgeous. You know that, right?"

"All I know right now is that my ass hurts."

"As it should after I've disciplined you. Your skin is the most beautiful shade of deep rose." Blaise snorted and received a hard smack. "Watch yourself, *brèagha*. I'm not sure who trained you, but he did a rotten job. You do not dispute my opinion on your loveliness."

She tried to hide her smile. Typical Dom. All the good ones she knew loved to see the pink or red of a well spanked ass, especially if they were the ones who'd caused it. She waited for her body to tense, for there to be an awkwardness before he indicated she could rise, but it didn't come. Instead, the relaxation he'd given her continued. Her body sagged across his thighs like a rag doll, and it took her a moment to realize her legs had relaxed and were now open, giving him a glimpse of her aroused response.

"And that is even more beautiful," he said, slipping his hand between her thighs. He seemed to hesitate, allowing her a chance to use a safeword.

Blaise knew what he could see because she could feel it. Her sex was swollen and glistened with arousal. He stroked her gently, the sound of his breathing becoming a bit ragged as his cock strained upward. Could it be that he was as affected by her as she was by him? She moaned as he dragged his finger from her labia to her clit and back again, touching her puckered rosette briefly.

"Has anyone taken you there?"

"No, Master. I never had any interest."

"I'll have to see if I can't persuade you about that as well."

"You have a lot of faith in your powers of seduction." She gasped as he penetrated her core with a single finger.

"Yes, I do," he said as he removed his fingers. She barely managed to stifle her cry of frustration. Drummond helped her to stand before turning her and pulling her onto his lap. "Relax, Blaise. You can stop me at any time, but I insist on a bit of aftercare."

He traced designs on her as he held her close to his body. It felt natural to relax against him, to allow her head to rest on his chest, to nuzzle his neck. There was something effortless about submitting to him. The man knew what he was doing. He chuckled, more to himself than as a true sound.

"What are you laughing about?"

"Mostly myself. You make me feel things I hadn't thought existed for me. Normally, I like my subs naked. I love women's bodies and I want easy access. Each of them has their own beauty and are so different from men's. And don't get me wrong, when it's just the two of us, you'll spend a lot of time without any clothes on, but I'd like to bind you so that your pussy is guarded and takes a bit of getting to.

Make no mistake, I'll get to it, but it might make for an interesting session."

"How often do you expect me to check in with you?" she asked.

"Check in? What part of twenty-four-seven do you not understand? This is no part-time or long-distance relationship. You'll live with me as my collared sub. You can work at the distillery, but for all intents and purposes you'll live with me."

"You said sex was..."

"To be negotiated," he reminded her. "And I also said I was going to do my best to get you to agree to be fucked and used sexually as often as I like. Have you ever lived in a D/s relationship with a Dom?"

"No, and I'm not sure I *want* to now."

"Then safeword out and we go to neutral corners, and you give up fifty-one percent of Kilted Fire to me permanently."

"You know I'm not going to do that. You want to put me over a barrel."

"Only to fuck or spank on occasion," he said, waggling his eyebrows at her.

Despite her best attempt not to, she laughed. He was going to be very hard to resist. Her pebbled nipples and dripping pussy combined with the thought of giving over and getting used on a regular basis sounded like a much better idea.

"I've gone over your hard and soft limits..."

"How would you know that? I didn't complete my

application for your club..." she said, relaxation fading as quickly as it had come.

"Easy, *brèagha*. You filled out most of it online. And, Fitzwallace is an old friend. I told him I was preparing a contract for you..."

"I thought you said you didn't know what was in my grandfather's will until this morning."

"I didn't, which should tell you a lot. I wanted this and was planning to get you to agree before I knew your grandfather would provide me with the leverage I needed."

Unsure of what to say, Blaise chose to say nothing.

CHAPTER 13

There was a soft knock on the door that broke the spell. As Blaise tried to get up, he held her in place.

"Not until I give you permission," he said, sternly.

"Can I at least pull up my jeans?"

He nodded and helped her to stand, watching as she pulled her jeans back up over her well-colored backside. Gavan didn't say anything; he didn't have to. Blaise settled herself back in his lap just as the knock came again.

"Come in," he called.

Vera stuck her head in and smiled. "I hate to disturb you two, but Craig and the Chief are here. Apparently, Tommy told Craig that Blaise had some suspicions about the fire."

"Damn," said Blaise, but quickly added, "That doesn't count as swearing."

"I determine what constitutes swearing deserving of discipline. You apologize and ask if that's a word that will earn you five before you use it."

"Fine. I'm sorry I said it. Can that please not be considered a curse word?"

"Good girl," he purred. "I'll consider letting it go in certain circumstances. Now why would Tommy tell Craig anything and why did it bother you?"

"Tommy and Craig are in a relationship. I said something to Tommy not thinking he'd say something to him. I should have known better."

"Why don't you want them to know?"

"Because I have zero hard evidence. Like you, I could smell the accelerant and I knew I'd made sure the stills were safe for the night." Blaise glanced at Vera.

"Speaking of which, you'll need to show the two men who'll be patrolling close to the house how to do that."

"That's my responsibility." Her attention snapped back to him.

"Nay, *brèagha*. You heard me. You're not to be outside or away from my side after nightfall."

"You don't have a signed contract yet," she said.

"I don't need one and we both know it, but you'll take five the next time you threaten me with that. Clear?"

"Yes, Sir."

"Then let's go see what the gentlemen want, and

I'd just as soon not invite them to stick their noses in until we know more."

He helped Blaise up. As she walked out the door past Vera she said, "Quit smirking." She might have said more, but Drummond smacked her bottom. "Ouch!"

"Vera is a Domme and a member of my club. You will be respectful."

Vera laughed. "I'm so glad I'm going to be around. This is going to be so fun to watch."

"You're supposed to be on my side," groused Blaise.

"Oh, but I am, dear. It's just the number one rule between Doms is never come between a Dom or Domme and his or her sub." She turned to Drummond. "I'd wipe that smile off my face if I were you. The jury's still out on whether or not you can tame her to your hand."

Drummond was still chuckling as they entered the sitting room.

"I was surprised to see your Range Rover here as we rolled up," said the Chief of the Fire and Rescue Service. "I wasn't aware you had business interests at Kilted Fire."

"Neither was I until the solicitor told me Lachlan had left me fifty-one percent of the business," he said, wrapping his arm around Blaise. "Plus, we've been keeping our relationship on the down low, but with Lachlan's death, we decided life was too short. Isn't that right, *brèagha*?"

"Right. Would you gentlemen like to sit down and tell us what this is all about? We have coffee and some delicious pastries. Would you care for some?"

Gavan was a bit surprised at how easily Blaise fell into the gracious hostess role.

"No, ma'am. That won't be necessary. This is a confidential investigation," said the chief.

"Really? Confidential from whom? After all, you wouldn't have known unless Craig told you, and he wouldn't have known if Tommy hadn't told him and on and on. Who in this room do you think we should keep this confidential from?"

He knew he should rein her back in, but watching her go after the officious little prick and Tommy's lover at the same time was far too much fun.

The chief sputtered. "Well, I suppose from Mr. Drummond and this woman."

"*This woman* is Vera McDonald who retired from Scotland Yard and was my grandfather's beloved companion. She will be living here at the house. As Gavan just told you, he is now a partner in Kilted Fire. I assure you chief, I trust both of them implicitly and anything you would say to me can be said to or in front of them."

Clearly rebuked, the chief ducked his head. "My apologies, but I do wonder why it is you chose not to tell us about your suspicions."

"Because," said Gavan stepping in, "We only had

vague suspicions based on nothing more than Blaise's experience with the stills. And while that's certainly enough for me to have our security patrol doubled and the system upgraded, neither of us thought it was enough to take you away from your other duties." *Duties*, which as far as Gavan could see, included playing cards and checkers with his friends, eating free meals provided by the restaurants in town, and collecting his salary. "Do you have information you'd like to share with us?"

"No, not really," said the chief. "I just wanted to know if you knew anything and if you thought we needed to open an attempted arson investigation."

"I don't think that's necessary. Do you, sweetheart?" he said, pulling Blaise close, a little surprised when she curled into him so easily.

"No, but if we come across anything substantial, we'll be sure to let you know." Blaise was all smiles with her reply.

"Gentlemen, why don't I show you out?" said Vera, gesturing toward the front door.

After they left, Blaise looked up at him. "We're doubling our security patrol? That's kind of overkill, don't you think?"

"No, I don't. I've already done it. We have the two men you requested, and I have two more patrolling the perimeter. By the way, they checked all of your fences and couldn't find where anyone got in, which means they either scaled the fence, which isn't the best idea, or they came down the drive."

"Do you think someone would be that bold?" she asked.

"Not so bold if they are seen here on a regular basis."

"What do you mean?"

"If it's a car or a bike or a motorcycle you or others are used to seeing here, it probably wouldn't even register. The brain would just see it and dismiss it as nothing special."

"You seem to know a lot about this."

Gavan nodded. "I do. It's called hiding in plain sight."

Vera rejoined them. "I don't think the chief was very happy with either of you."

"The chief's happiness isn't an issue I concern myself with," said Gavan dismissively.

"Maybe, but he can make things difficult for us," said Blaise. "Granda always felt it was better to appease him."

Gavan looked at her sharply. "Appease? As in pay him off?"

Blaise shrugged. "It's cheaper than the fines he could levy."

"That stops now."

"Really? The gangster who regularly extorts money from businesses for his protection is going to sneer at the local fire chief who does the same?"

"It is entirely different and is something I only do in Inverness."

"Well, that would make all the difference," said Blaise.

"I do not need to justify my business to you."

"I suppose not. Speaking of business, I have one to run, or at least forty-nine percent of it to run."

Without waiting for him to say anything, Blaise walked out the front door, leaving Gavan alone with Vera.

"She doesn't know much about you, does she?" asked Vera.

"No and seems inclined to believe the worst," he said, looking after her distractedly.

"Why not tell her the truth?"

Gavan whipped around to face her. "What truth might that be?"

There were few outside the clan who knew of their true nature as shifters who could morph between their human selves and those of their animal selves. After all, black tigers had been extinct in the highlands for a millennia.

"That while you are the head of the Galloglass Syndicate, you do far more good than harm. You and your compatriots: Knight, O'Neill, and Hughes seem to work together."

He breathed a silent sigh of relief. It was bad enough that the cunning retired cop had figured out the four of them were connected, but far less dangerous than if she'd known the truth about his kind.

"Friends yes, but compatriots? You make it sound more like co-conspirators."

"Oh, I'm sure you're a rather friendly bunch, but I always thought that there was more to it than that. All four syndicates have some unusual similarities."

"I'm curious. Such as?"

"None of you trades in drugs. In fact, you all keep them out of your territories and will go after anyone who tries either to deal drugs or smuggle them through. O'Neill and Hughes have no connections to hookers and while you and Knight do, it's more of a benevolent attitude. I know that all four of you have been known to help the police in the right circumstances and my old boss once said none of you had ever killed anyone who didn't need killing. I'm sure there's a whole lot more, but I'm retired and more than that, I know who you are at your core, so your secrets are safe with me."

"I'm glad to hear it," he said with a smile.

"I was surprised to hear Blaise had agreed to a contract."

"I didn't give her much choice. If she wants my fifty-one percent at the end of a year, she has to be my sub for that length of time."

"I don't believe you. You are not a manipulative Dom, and you often show a decided dislike of those who are. You were going to give her back the company at the end of the year anyway, weren't you?"

"I don't know, Vera, that sounds fairly manipulative to me."

"Yes and no. I think you know how she feels, probably better than she does."

"And how is that?"

"Instinctively, she knows she needs a strong Dom, but she's not ready to admit it. I know Lachlan always hoped the two of you would find your way to each other. When he knew he was dying, he just decided to give you a little push. So even though you'd have given the company to her anyway, you used it to honor Lachlan's wishes and see if you couldn't show her how good her life could be with the right partner."

"Again, more than just a bit manipulative, don't you think?"

"Maybe. If you were planning to abuse her or treat her badly, but you won't. Sometimes a good Dom has to be creative in helping their sub come to the right solution."

He laughed. "So, you're saying I'm creative, not manipulative."

"Exactly. Will you give her a collar?"

"And a ring to go with it. I had both made for her earlier this year."

Vera sat down on the settee. "I have to say that I didn't see that coming. You're going to need to make her right with your other business. You can't keep things from her."

"I will keep her safe, and if that means keeping her in the dark about certain aspects of my life, so be it."

Vera shook her head. "Don't do it, Gavan. You and I both know D/s doesn't work without good communication and absolute truth."

"I'll remind you that how I conduct my D/s relationship is really none of your business and as you pointed out to Blaise, one Dom doesn't come between another and his sub."

"To a point. If I ever think you're abusing her or don't have her best interests at heart, I'll bring you before your own council at Termonn."

He should have seen that coming. Gavan had instituted a council of the Doms who held Master's level rights at the club after one Dom had flown under the radar and had badly damaged a girl. Gavan had stepped in, almost killing the man, and forcing him to flee the UK. In order to ensure it didn't happen again, he instituted stricter safety protocols and had created a council where any member, sub or Dom, could bring another member up before the council. He had no doubt that Vera wouldn't hesitate to do just that.

"I would expect no less," said Gavan.

He wanted complete honesty and transparency with Blaise. He wanted her to be his true partner in everything. Gavan wanted what O'Neill had with his

Katy, the beautiful undercover agent who'd almost brought him down, faked her own death, then come back to him. He'd have to remember to buy O'Neill a drink. Afterall, it was his bargain with Katy that had brought them back together. Maybe lightning could strike twice in the same way and his pact with Blaise would produce the same result. What was the old saying? *Hope Springs Eternal.* He hoped it was that one and not *Man Plans and God Laughs*. Why not? If it worked for the Devil of Galway, perhaps it could work for the Black Tiger of Skye.

CHAPTER 14

The hours dragged by. It felt as though she hadn't done anything right all day. Normal things she did without thinking were taking twice as long and even then, they needed to be done over. She couldn't focus. Her mind seemed to be filled with thoughts and now memories of Gavan Drummond. She wondered if she'd ever be able to go into the study or the storeroom and not be overwhelmed by images of the two encounters she'd had in those rooms.

Blaise tried to banish the mental distractions that threatened to overwhelm her, especially in light of the fact that she knew there would be more, and not just spankings—although she was certain there'd be more of those as well. She knew playing at his club would be intense, but that wasn't what worried her. What caused her the most concern was that she would get far too much pleasure out of them, become far too dependent on Drummond, and be crushed when it was all over.

A collar. She'd never been collared by a Dom. She wasn't sure she wanted to be, but Drummond had been firm on that. She'd been asked more than once, although she suspected in the last few years more to get her to have intercourse with them than any real emotional connection. So why was Drummond so insistent? She wondered what it looked like. Did it matter? After all, a year from now, she'd be returning it.

As the sun's light began to diminish, Blaise wandered the floors of the drying kiln houses, checking the humidity of the malted barley. When she checked the same batch for the fourth time, Tommy said, "What the hell is wrong with you?"

"Me?" she said, spinning on her feet and crowding his personal space. "I told you about my suspicions about the fire in confidence. I didn't expect you to go blabbing to your boyfriend."

"Well, you didn't tell me not to…"

"I guess I thought you were smarter than that. For your information, Craig then went to his boss, and I had to handle the situation with him and the chief this morning. Not my idea of a fun time."

"I would think telling them everything you know and allowing them to investigate would be the best way to handle the situation," Tommy said, his voice rising in anger.

"Good thing for me you're not the one making the decisions."

"Maybe not, but I heard you aren't either."

They stood glaring at each other. So, word had already spread about her grandfather's will. Drummond had agreed not to interfere with the day-to-day operations, but could she trust that he would actually follow through on that? For the first time in her life, Blaise didn't know what to do. She'd been an instinctive leader for as long as she could remember. It had surprised her when she'd discovered how deeply submissive she could be, almost seemed contradictory. Until she'd started going to Baker Street and realized there were a lot of submissives like her: powerful and in control in their daily life, but who needed to release that control in order to relax and be completely satisfied.

Blaise could feel Drummond behind her and turned to face him. "What do you want?"

"It's getting to be the end of the day, *brèagha*. You either need to start banking the stills for the night or tell the two security guys when and how to do it."

"I can do that, Mr. Drummond," offered Tommy brightly from behind Blaise.

Well, wasn't that just ducky. The guy she'd thought she could count on was already trying to go around her straight to Drummond.

"Not my call. The Munro still runs Kilted Fire," Drummond said solemnly.

Blaise looked at him and blinked back tears. The fact that he'd not usurped her authority and had then called her by an ancient title that indicated she was in charge both surprised and bolstered her. True, the Munros weren't of the nobility, but they were landed gentry—those who owned land but had no title to pass along to their children.

Calmly, she turned back to Tommy. "Why don't you just do your job, Tommy, and check the kilns and the malting barns. Gavan, it may take a wee bit longer, but I can show the guys tonight as I do it and maybe supervise them doing it tomorrow. I know you wanted to leave by sundown."

"That will work. We'll be later than I'd like, but I'll let you make it up to me when we get home."

Home? What the hell did he mean by home? She was home.

"I've shown Vera how to set the alarms, and we can let the boys know she's up at the house by herself for the night. I asked her if she wanted us to send someone down to be with her," said Gavan deferentially, but firmly.

She did like the way he kept saying *we* and *us,* but if Vera was going to be alone, where the hell was she going to be? She knew her face must show confusion, but the light dawned for her and with it, Drummond smiled. He was taking her home to Castle Cat-Sith with him and she very much doubted she'd be shown to a guest room.

"She assured me she'd be fine and would have a handgun on the night table beside her, but still I think we should hire a housekeeper for her, don't you?" he asked in a loving tone.

"Uhm, yes."

She'd made this deal with him. He would hold to his word about no sex and still play and scene with her. After all, she'd agreed to be his sub. Somehow, she also knew without a doubt that he would honor her safewords and the pact they'd made.

Dismissing Tommy completely, Drummond continued, "The boys should be here shortly and will meet us at the stillhouse. Make sure you bring your phone with you so we can upgrade the security app tonight." He raised his face to look Tommy in the eye. "Good to see you again, Tommy. I hope that in the future you'll respect the confidentiality of what goes on here. I think Blaise needs to be able to trust her right-hand man."

"Absolutely, Mr. Drummond. My apologies to you both. It won't happen again."

She was really going to have to get him to teach her how to do that. He'd put Tommy in his place and on notice and done both without ever making her look weak. When Drummond opened his arm to her, she didn't even hesitate in joining him, wrapping her arm around his waist as he closed his around her shoulders.

When they were out of earshot she said, "I am sorry about the time. I should have kept a closer eye on it. I wasn't expecting to leave with you tonight."

"I told you last night that when I left here, I would have you by my side. I am not a man given to making idle conversation."

"I know. I just hadn't extrapolated it all the way out. I also want to thank you for how you handled Tommy."

"He was out of line, and he needs to know, so he can tell the others, that *nothing* has changed in how Kilted Fire is run." He squeezed her side gently as if to punctuate the honesty of his words. "Did you have a chance to look at the books?"

"They're up in the study and I wanted to be seen in the works today. They're going to take some looking at. Granda kept most of the figures and what he knew in his head."

"I have every confidence in you," he rumbled soothingly to her.

Why was it that his very presence held comfort and safety and his praise was quickly coming to mean more to her than she'd ever thought it would?

"If you need someone to help you, short-term or permanently, we can hire whoever you need. I don't want you to think that you have to take on both yours and your grandfather's responsibilities."

"That's the thing. I don't even feel like I know enough about what he did to try and hire someone."

"I wish I could help more. I can help explain some financial matters if you need because a balance sheet is a balance sheet, but all I know about whisky distillers is which brand of scotch is my preference."

"And that would be?" she teased.

"Kilted Fire, of course."

They met with the two security guards. They were not what she'd pictured in her mind. For some reason, she'd thought they'd be kind of slight and meek as though they couldn't find a job as a real cop or a soldier. Both men looked like poster boys for a black ops mercenary group, and they were surprisingly smart and quick learners. When they left, the sky had darkened from the sun's disappearance beyond the western horizon, but the moon had yet to reach its high point. Yet, she still felt comfortable.

"Vera packed a bag for you, and I put it in the Range Rover."

"They weren't what I expected," she said. He eyed her with an unspoken question. "I thought they'd be kind of wimpy, but when I saw they were beefcakes, I thought they'd be dumb. They were neither and seemed to really care."

"In the spirit of honesty, they work for me. It's Dougal's company and he pays their salary and all the associated taxes, but they were originally on my payroll. For me, muscle without the intelligence to back it up is just asking for trouble."

"Is Dougal's company a front for your organization?" she asked.

He laughed. "No, and he's not laundering money for me either. Did I invest in Dougal's company? Yes. Do I own a very small percentage of it? Yes. But Dougal runs his own show. I like being able to help entrepreneurs but more than that, I like having people make money for me."

He helped her into his vehicle and she all but sighed, running her hands over the rich leather interior.

"Okay, now I'm getting jealous of my SUV," he said.

"I've always wanted one of these babies. I think they're gorgeous and they handle so well. I got upgraded to one when I had to rent a car one time. It's my dream car. I think about manifesting it when I find the time to meditate."

"If you want a Range Rover, Blaise, we'll go pick one out for you. If you won't accept it as a gift from me, we can buy it as a company vehicle. I was going to talk to you about your truck at some point. It really is a piece of crap. If I can't talk you into letting me dispose of it, I will insist that one of my mechanics goes over it and every single thing that needs to be fixed gets done."

"That truck was my grandfather's. Here," she

said, extending her arm to him. "Twist it so I can say you forced me to get a Kilted Fire Range Rover."

Drummond laughed. "I arranged your grandfather's celebration at the club for the night after next. There's a dealership in Inverness. Why don't we take the day, and we can go in and order one. If you can think of anything else the distillery needs, make a list and we'll either pick it up or order it."

"I don't know that I can do it that quickly. I really don't know what our cash situation is."

"I appreciate that, but I have the cash and can loan the distillery the money. The company can pay me back whenever you're ready."

"Only if it's a loan."

"Scout's honor." He held up his fingers.

Blaise barked a laugh. "You were never in the Scouts Scotland, were you?"

"No," he said sheepishly. "But it sounded good, and you can determine how you want to classify the money when you do the books."

"By the way, I appreciate you calling me 'The Munro.'"

"It's the truth. With your grandfather gone, you are The Munro."

"Well, I wanted you to know I noticed, and it did make me feel good."

"That's part of a good Dom's job, *brèagha*. Praising his sub for a job well done and making her feel good."

"Don't think I didn't notice how you put Tommy

in his place and backed me up when it would have been easier to just take over."

"Easier? Maybe, but not better. Keep in mind that I have my own enterprises to run, but I want you to know I will do whatever you need me to do."

CHAPTER 15

here was something about the intimacy of being on the road with someone at night. Castle Cat-Sith was only thirty minutes from Kilted Fire if it was daylight and you were driving at the speed limit, but neither of those conditions applied. He was being selfish, not being a very good Dom. She had to be exhausted from the emotional turmoil of the day alone, but she'd had two discipline sessions and a hard fuck in less than twenty-four hours, and he meant to have her again tonight. Granted, he'd need to persuade her, but given the way she responded to him, he didn't see that as much of an obstacle.

The road was dark. This stretch had no streetlights, and the night was overcast. He kept his eyes focused on the lanes ahead, splitting his roving glances between her and the rearview mirror. At least there was no one behind him trying to get by. It was a lonely stretch of road, but it meant he didn't have to be in a hurry.

As his eyes swept the view out his back window, he thought he caught a glimpse of something. He continued driving, said nothing to her, but began dividing his attention more fully between what was in front of them and what he was concerned might be behind. Hamish had long wanted him to have at least one bodyguard with him at all times, but Gavan felt that was kind of wimpy. However, for the next year, or hopefully longer, he was inclined to change his stance. Right now he'd have given anything for one of the boys to be sitting in the back seat.

There it was again. No light, but the movement of a shadow that shouldn't have been there. He gripped the steering wheel a little tighter and looked to ensure Blaise was buckled in. She wasn't.

"Buckle up. Now," he growled in a voice she would know didn't brook any conversation or disobedience. "Don't let me catch you in a car without one. If I do, I'll make sure you can't sit comfortably for a week. Got it?"

Ignoring his angry tone, Blaise buckled her seatbelt, before asking, "What's wrong?"

"Maybe nothing."

"But maybe not?"

He nodded. "I think someone may be behind us. I don't want to have to take my eyes off the road in front or in back. Can you activate my phone? It's synced with the vehicle. It'll bring up a list of contacts. Call Hamish."

Quietly and efficiently, she did as he asked, and Hamish answered. "What's up? You headed back here with your lady?"

"Yes. You're on speaker and she can hear you so mind what you say."

"Not a problem. Hi, Blaise."

"Hello, Hamish."

"What's up, boss?"

"I think someone might be following us. I could be paranoid, but I don't want to take any chances. We're about halfway between Kilted Fire and the castle."

"I'll get our people to you. I'll send an SUV both from here and the distillery and I'll get the chopper up in the air."

"You have a helicopter?" she asked.

"We do. Have you ever ridden in one?"

"No."

"Well, hopefully that won't change tonight, but if you'd like to go for a ride, we can. We can take it to Inverness."

"Boss, you can plan your date later. Keep driving nice and steady. Don't give any indication you've spotted them. The SUVs should have you in sight in fifteen or less. I'm in the chopper; we should be there in less than seven."

The call ended and he removed one hand from

the wheel to reach over and squeeze hers. "I'll take care of you."

Blaise took his hand and squeezed back. "I know."

Looking in the rearview mirror, he saw nothing, but that didn't comfort him. Just because he couldn't see it, didn't mean someone wasn't out there looking to do him harm. There was no doubt in his mind that someone had started that fire at the distillery. He'd spent his day in the study of the house monitoring what Blaise was up to and running deep background checks on all of her employees. He was convinced one of them was the culprit but was still unsure as to why.

Still, whoever was behind them might have nothing to do with the fire. They might, quite literally, be gunning for him, and that was what really worried him. They would be trapped between two vehicles with no place to go and be subjected to a barrage of gunfire. He didn't want to frighten her, but he needed her to be aware and maybe she could help him keep an eye on things.

"Without unbuckling, can you twist in your seat and look out the back window?"

She did as he asked. "What am I looking for?"

"A shadow that shouldn't be there. I hope to God when Hamish gets here, he gets to have a big laugh at my expense. Whatever I or Hamish tells you to do, you do it. You don't ask questions, you don't hesitate, you just do it."

"Yes, Master. I really can't see anything. Damn the

clouds. None of the moon or stars are getting through."

He was amazed by her level of calm. He almost thought she was used to this kind of thing.

"You seem pretty unphased by all of this."

"I see no reason to panic. For one thing, it won't help anyone, and for another, you said you'd keep me safe, and I believe you."

She had no way of knowing what that meant to him. He wasn't sure what had caused it or when, but he felt as though they'd taken a large step forward in their relationship.

"Thank you, *brèagha*. That means a great deal to me."

"I still can't—no wait. I can see something. I think it's gaining on us."

"I need you to turn back around and brace for impact. They may try to run us off the road."

"That's not good. On the seaward side, there's a sheer drop off."

He felt the hit from behind as the large vehicle behind them turned on its high beams and rammed into the bumper. Gavan didn't speed up or slow down. He focused on the road ahead since his rearview mirror was of no use as all he could see was a blinding white light.

The Range Rover jolted forward as they were slammed from behind again. This time they didn't hit them square on, but from the driver's side, which forced their vehicle dangerously close to the edge. He knew there was a dirt road just ahead. Gavan pressed the accelerator, hoping to get them to safety.

The men in the vehicle behind them were professionals. They kept pace, coming abreast of them, ramming into the Range Rover a third time from the side. Gavan glanced up to see their assailant's back window come down and the muzzle of a gun being leveled at him.

"Hold tight! This is going to get bumpy," he said as he grabbed the wheel tighter and swerved off the road.

Even though the Range Rover was built for rough terrain, it was taking all of his considerable strength and driving ability to keep from flipping the vehicle and sending them rolling down the side of the rocky sea wall. The high beams stayed at the top of the hill, but he could hear three vehicle doors opening. Their attackers were in pursuit.

When they came to a stop, Gavan hit the accelerator, hoping the tires could find purchase and he could get them moving forward. If they could make the hard-pack sand, they might be able to put enough distance between them and the gunmen to use the vehicle for protection until Hamish could arrive with help. The wheels spun and moved them nowhere.

"Out!" he ordered, glad to see that Blaise's composure was still intact.

They were both out of the vehicle, but their

assailants were closing in. Grabbing her hand, he darted to the right, getting them out of the beam of the Range Rover's headlamps and away from the path that led down to the beach. They ran across the rugged landscape, listening for their pursuers. They weren't disappointed because Gavan felt the zing of a bullet graze his upper arm.

As they continued to run, Gavan said, "I want you to run a zig-zag pattern back up the hill."

"I'm not leaving you."

"You'll do as you're told. I need you to obey me. Once you get to the road, run toward Castle Cat-Sith. Hamish will see you and pick you up and you can direct him back to my location. I'm going to try and lead them away from you and down to the ocean. The only way we get out of this alive is if my men get here."

"I don't know that I believe you, but I don't have a better idea. My experience with people trying to kill me is not nearly as extensive as yours. Stay alive, Drummond. I need that fifty-one percent."

She let go of his hand and darted away. Once she'd crested the first dune, Gavan found a place to crouch down. It wouldn't give him much protection for long, but it would have to be enough. Quickly, he stripped out of his clothes and called to his tiger, who'd been waiting for his chance to take these bastards on. The sliver of moon barely alleviated the total darkness. The faint shimmer went hazy and warped as it bent its magick around him and Gavan and the black tiger became one.

He charged over the dune and was surprised to see the gunmen were not where he'd expected them to be. Instead of pursuing him, they'd turned to chase down Blaise. That would prove to be a fatal choice on their part. Gavan galloped after them, closing the distance in seconds. He avoided any intersection of light and dark. His night vision had sharpened with the emergence of his primal beast. The spit of a handgun firing in her direction caught his most immediate attention and he charged. The gunman heard his rush at the last second and turned to fire, but was too late. Gavan grasped his skull between his powerful jaws and crunched, killing him instantly.

Tossing the corpse aside, he ran toward the next assassin. *Damn it. Where was Hamish?* The thought had no more formed than he heard a volley of gunfire and saw the running lights of the chopper switch on as he heard the *whoosh! whoosh! whoosh!* of the blades cutting through the night air. He could see the helicopter overhead with its search light directed toward them.

There was another burst of automatic gunfire, but this time coming from the helicopter and aimed at those who'd tried to kill them. He could make out men jumping out of the helicopter as it hovered close to the road. Gavan didn't realize he'd been holding his breath until his men reached her and she pointed toward where he'd run. That was his cue to get back to his clothes and get dressed. He hoped to God they weren't all dead so he'd have an assailant to question… and torture. Someone was going to pay for this and if he found out that the attack had been directed at Blaise, he'd rain hellfire down on whoever had perpetrated it.

Once he was dressed, he went back to the wrecked Range Rover. The phone was ringing, and he leaned inside to hit the answer button.

"We got 'em boss. Your lady is in the helicopter with Hamish. We have two of them."

"There was a third. We'll need to dispose of the body. I killed him between your position and the ocean."

"Got it. Hamish wants the chopper to put down on the beach, pick you up and get you to the castle. He's not sure of the sand so they'll hover right above the ground. Hamish will join us to get things cleaned up, then meet you back at the Castle."

Gavan found the dirt path that led down to the strip of beach where Hamish was waiting. His second ducked under the rotor blades and came to meet him, followed closely by Blaise. He had no doubt Hamish had told her to stay put, but his mate wasn't inclined to do as she was told. She needed to learn that in a dangerous situation, there would be hell to pay for not doing so.

"Hello, my Master," she said sweetly.

She was either up to something, just being terribly

polite and trying to make up for her lack of obedi-
ence, or in shock. He only hoped it wasn't the latter.
He had a rush of adrenaline he'd like to work off with
her, but if she was really frightened, he'd need to take
care of her first.

"Are you all right? Blaise?" Gavan spoke to
Hamish but looked directly at Blaise.

"We're both fine. You?" his second answered.

"I am now. You get one I told you so. I want at
least six men up at the distillery tonight. Two inside
the house, two on the main ground, and two
patrolling the perimeter. Put the castle on high alert.
I'll call Vera and let her know you're coming."

"You think they're after you or her?"

"Doesn't matter. I want any survivors patched up
and locked in the dungeon. I'm going to take Blaise
home and make sure she's all right. We can talk in the
morning."

Before getting on the chopper, he called Vera to
alert her to what had happened.

"I can handle myself, Gavan," said the Domme.

"I'm sure you can, but I need to be able to tell
Blaise that you're safe. She's not going to let me take
care of her if she has any doubt that you're in
danger."

"Any of your people hurt?"

"No. Hamish would have told me."

"I take it we're not calling the police," she said
sardonically.

"This part of *we* sure as hell isn't. I mean to find out who and what they were after and shut them down. Coming after me and mine is never a smart thing to do."

"I suppose this would be a case of them deserving whatever happens to them." He could almost hear her smirk through the phone.

"Damn straight." He hung up when she mumbled a goodbye and said the same.

Wrapping his arm around Blaise's waist, he led her toward the helicopter.

"Vera?"

She was too smart by half. "Fine and I've increased security. Let's get in the chopper and go home. I'll have the chopper lift up and fly the stretch of beach. If it scares you too much, we can make other arrangements."

Blaise held onto his hand, only the strength of her grip indicating she was afraid. So much for working off his adrenaline.

"I'll be fine. As long as you're with me, I'll be all right."

"Good girl," he said, brushing his lips over hers and tamping down his need to crush her to him. "Keep your head down."

He helped her into the rear seat of the chopper, so that she was sitting between him and one of his security people while the remaining security guy took the seat next to the pilot. They lifted off and Blaise held on tight. When he looked at her, she smiled and gave him a thumbs up. She was amazing.

His pilot must have guessed by Blaise's demeanor that she'd never flown in a chopper because he took it nice and easy. Their route back to the castle was slow and steady, landing on their helipad where burly men with two SUVs were waiting.

As soon as they cleared the rotor blades, they were met by a member of the clan. "Hamish called. They had six men, a driver and two men in each SUV. One driver and one shooter survived. A little banged up but nothing life threatening. Nessa said she would have dinner taken up to your room. She figured you wouldn't want to subject Ms. Munro to dinner at the castle after what happened."

"I don't want anyone to go to any trouble on my account..." started Blaise.

"It's no trouble, *brèagha*. Give Nessa my thanks and have dinner sent up in an hour. Unless, Blaise, are you hungry now?"

"Not hungry per se, but I could use a drink and probably shouldn't do that on an empty stomach."

"You heard the lady. Please have Nessa send us something to munch on. I keep a bottle of hundred-year-old Kilted Fire in my bedroom."

"Who'd you have to kill for that?" she quipped.

"I'll have you know that your grandfather sent it to me the night he asked me to watch over you, Vera, and the distillery."

"I still don't understand that. He knew Vera and I were both capable and he asked you to come before the fire."

Gavan looked at her. "That is interesting. Let's get inside; and we'll talk about it more when we're up in our rooms."

"Rooms, as in separate?"

"What's the matter Blaise? Disappointed? But no, ours is the master suite that looks out over the sea. It consists of a bedroom, sitting area, bath and we have our own private outdoor space."

As they entered Castle Cat-Sith, a cheer went up. The foyer inside the main doors was impressive, as was the sweeping staircase that led to the upper floors. He realized just before they got to the bottom of the stairs that whatever had been keeping her upright and propelling her forward, had deserted her. He caught her just as her knees began to buckle.

Cradling her to his chest, he started up the stairs. "I've got you, *brèagha*. I've got you."

CHAPTER 16

*H*e carried her into the room, shushing her when she protested feebly, not so much he thought at sharing his room, but at being carried and fussed over. She was going to have to get used to that. He loved the feel of her in his arms.

"I'm fine, Gavan."

"Yes, you are," he said, noticing it was the first time she'd called him by his given name. "I'm going to sit you here by the balcony while I grab a quick shower. When they bring up the appetizers, they'll knock—just tell them to come in. I want you sitting here when I come out of the bath."

"I'm not made of porcelain," she grumbled.

"God, I hope not because I'll break you when I fuck you." She laughed. That was a good sign. "Behave yourself."

"Yes, Master," she said in a way that couldn't be faulted, but that failed to hide her amusement.

Within a few minutes, he was stripped out of his clothes and stepping into as cold a shower as he could manage. He needed to get a tight grip on his growing arousal. His blood was running hot and as a black tiger-shifter, it already ran hotter than a human's. Gavan figured if he handled things right and was reading Blaise correctly, she'd be in his bed and beneath him some time this evening. He just had to make sure it was because she wanted to be, not because she felt obligated.

Who the fuck cares why she's there? said his cock, which had developed a mind of its own. It didn't care if she was scared, obligated or horny, it wanted back inside her desperately. More than that, it wanted him to allow his barbs to cover the surface of his shaft so he could make her yowl while he fucked her hard and long.

The cold shower didn't eradicate the problem, but at least it wasn't throbbing quite as painfully as before, and he felt as though he had a better handle on his libido. He pulled on a pair of sweatpants. All that control flew out the window, or in this case the French doors, when he entered the bedroom to find a naked Blaise kneeling on the floor. Her head was bowed, her eyes lowered, and her fiery red curls floated around her shoulders. Placed beside her was the bottle of scotch and two tumblers with the tray of appetizers in her hands, raised in front of her as an offering.

He was glad now he hadn't berated Fitzwallace for her training. She was perfect. She was waiting quietly for his command, knowing full well where that would lead. His cock came back to a painful state of being. This was not the first time he'd found a sub waiting for him with some kind of offering, but always at the club, never here at the castle. She would be the only woman to ever grace his bed.

Gavan took the tray from her, placing it and the spirits on the table next to the wingback chair overlooking the sea. He smiled, remembering what she'd felt like this morning over his knee as he'd sat in the study, administering his discipline. She didn't raise her head even an inch. "You are exquisite, Blaise. I'm assuming it's more than food and scotch you're offering me?"

"Yes, Master."

He walked over to the hidden safe, slid back the paneled wall, and opened it. Both the necklace case with her collar and the ring box were inside. He meant to collar her this evening, but he would give her a bit more time on the question of the ring. He returned to her and held out his hand. She'd placed both of hers on her thighs, palms up. Her red hair fell down her back, midway to her waist. She'd taken out the braid it had been in all day. She was gorgeous, taller than average and more strongly built. She was no petite will-of-the-wisp. She had a true hourglass figure with large, natural breasts, a nipped in waist and hips that flowed out, hips he had and would take hold of to keep her in place when he thrust hard inside her.

Gavan knew he should take the time to explain who and what he really was, how the syndicate fulfilled a role that had been passed down through his family for generation upon generation. The problem was he wouldn't risk not having her. He meant to bind her to him in as many ways as possible and given her passionate nature, that would include sex.

She took his hand and he helped her to her feet. Her movements were studied and graceful. Gavan was fairly sure she'd spent hours practicing. Who had she knelt before in the past? Probably best he didn't know as he wanted to kill him, them, or whoever he or they might be.

He lifted her chin. "Keep your eyes closed, Blaise, and turn around." She turned away from him. "If you like, we can have an actual collaring ceremony at the club, either at your grandfather's celebration or we can wait a few weeks, but I want my collar around your throat tonight."

Reaching into the pocket of his sweatpants, he pulled out the collar he'd had created especially for her. It was made of rare black Cairngorm Quartz crystal, the national gemstone found only in the Cairngorm Mountains of Scotland. Between the Cairngorm crystals were white diamonds mounted in a filigreed, sterling silver setting. The clasp was a small, intricate lock in the shape of a black tiger, to which only he had the key. While her eyes remained closed, Blaise instinctively reached up to touch the collar but stayed her hand when he growled low in his throat.

He led her to the small mirror that adorned the top of his antique tallboy dresser. "You can open your eyes now."

The small gasp that leapt from her mouth was all he needed to hear.

"Gavan, it's breathtaking and way too much."

"I'm glad you like it. I don't think it's nearly enough." Taking her by the hand, he led her to the chair. He prevented her from taking the seat at his side as he pulled her into his lap. "Nay, *brèagha*. This is where you belong."

He held her close, quietly rocking her as they shared the food and spirits. He was careful not to let her drink too much. Even so, she drifted off to sleep, so that when they brought dinner, Gavan was careful not to wake her. He made sure that whatever it was could be eaten cold. He had it set up on the dresser and asked that unless it was vitally important that they not be disturbed before ten.

When they were alone, he lifted his sleeping

beauty in his arms and carried her to the bed that had been turned down for them. Gavan deposited her in the bed and removed his sweatpants, silently chuckling as they got caught up on his erection before he could toss them over the footboard of the enormous sleigh bed. They'd have to get a different bed or install some elaborate restraint system. He rather preferred the spontaneity of having some kind of four poster iron bed so that he had many options for tying her up.

Crawling into bed next to her, he sighed contentedly as he pulled her close and she snuggled next to him as if they'd been together for years. His cock was complaining angrily that its pussy was so close. She'd said yes, but his cock would just have to wait... at least for a few hours. She was worth waiting for. He couldn't remember ever wanting anything or anyone the way he wanted her.

Several hours later, her sleep seemed disturbed by angry dreams. "Shhh, *brèagha*. I am here. All is well."

"Gavan?" she said sleepily. "Did I fall asleep? How did I get here?"

"From the chair to my bed or here at the castle? Do you remember what happened earlier?"

"Of course. We were driving down the coast road from the distillery to the castle. Some bad guys tried to run us off the road and you and your men saved us."

"You were very brave. I was so proud of you, and

not once did you question whether or not I would take care of you."

She rubbed her eyes. "It never entered my mind. After all, what good is it being the sub of a mafia boss if you can't trust him to triumph over the even more evil bad guys."

"Do you think I'm evil?"

"No," she said, shaking her head gently. "Not anymore. I don't want to think I'm giving a year of my life to some wicked, despicable gangster."

"And after a year?" he knew he shouldn't push, but this was too important.

"I don't know that it would be a good idea…"

"Give me a chance." He couldn't believe he was pleading, so he changed tactics and deepened his voice. "I'll make you believe. Before the year ends, you won't even remember that you ever questioned us."

Pulling her to him, he rolled her to her back and slipped his hand between her thighs to stroke her silky sex, drawing her honey up to her clit to rub it in. Blaise moaned and lifted her pelvis toward him. He took his hand away and she groaned.

"You know better, *brèagha*."

"Before last night, it had been a very, very long time and it was so good," she pleaded.

"I want you to stay still until I give you permission to move. Do you think you can do that for me?"

"Yes, Master."

She relaxed her body back into the mattress, and parted her legs, revealing visual proof of what his keen sense of smell had already told him was glistening at the opening to her core. She was already primed and ready for him: soft, wet, and swollen. He stroked her again, flicking his fingers over her distended clit before pressing down on it. She groaned once more in the sexiest way possible but was doing her best not to come.

"Is there something you want, *brèagha*?"

"Yes, please, Master. May I come?"

"Such a sweet and polite request. Do you want me to take you gently?"

"No, Master. Please?"

"You have to learn to ask me for what you want if it's something specific."

"No. I want you to fuck me hard like you did last night. Please."

"In a bit. I want a taste of you first."

He rolled over her, working his way down her body until he'd settled between her thighs. Swirling his tongue around her clit, he nipped her, the pain just enough to back her off from the orgasm that had been almost within her reach. Blaise writhed beneath his touch. He licked down her sex until he speared her pussy deeply, reveling in the way her sheath quivered from his touch. He reached back up to her clit with his hand and commanded her climax as he tugged on her little jewel sharply, driving his tongue back inside her, flattening it so he could lap up her orgasm as it coated his tongue.

As she rode the crest of her pleasure, he slithered up her body, never removing himself from between her legs. She welcomed him with open arms that closed around him as he settled on her, bearing his weight. She was strong enough to handle him and soft enough to yield. The head of his cock was poised against her opening as he began to press into her. She was tight; he remembered that from the last time. His cock also reminded him of the way her cunt milked it as he came. It was beyond anything he'd ever felt before.

Gavan dragged himself back, then drove deep, making her gasp from his penetration. He pulled almost all the way out before thrusting back in, two, three, four times. He focused on her pleasure and her response, taking strong, measured strokes as he fucked her hard. His hands slipped beneath her, cupping her ass and holding her in place. Over and over, he slammed his pelvis into her, driving deep each time until her orgasm burst forth with such ferocity that it washed over and consumed them both.

With one last brutal push, he drove into her, holding himself hard against her body as wave after wave of cum spewed forth, filling her to capacity and beyond. When it was over, he collapsed on top of her, basking in the way her body cushioned his. A deep satisfaction he'd never known flooded his system. He snuggled against her for just a moment before rolling off and pulling her close as he did so.

Her deep, even breathing came almost immediately. They would sign a contract in two days, and he meant to ensure that she wanted sex included. He vowed to himself that regardless of what happened at the end of the year, he would never give her up.

CHAPTER 17

S he woke just as the sun started to clear the horizon, foggy from the lack of sleep and overabundance of sex. And not just any sex, but spectacular sex with Gavan Drummond. Her hand went up to her throat.

"It's still there. You should know, I've thrown away the key. If you want it off, you'll have to have it cut off and if someone is looking, they'll realize the black tiger is a symbol I use frequently."

"In other words, they'll be too afraid to do it."

"That's the idea. Are you ready to wake up?"

"Yes. What time is it?"

"It's early yet. Besides, it won't take but about fifteen minutes by helicopter. Vera called a little bit ago. She wanted to know if I'd learned anything. The answer is not yet. If you're determined to go to the distillery..."

"I'm The Munro, remember?" she teased.

"All too well," he snickered. "In that case, I'm going to send Hamish and two more men with you. Neither you nor Vera go anywhere alone until we find out what's going on."

"That's a bit of overkill, don't you think?"

"Kill being the operative word. Those guys weren't playing last night. They were a professional assassination squad. That's expensive. By the way, thank you for last night. I needed to work off that adrenaline."

She was taken a little aback but tried to hide it. Was that all it had been to him? Just a way to unwind after someone had tried to kill them?

"I wouldn't like what you're thinking right now, would I?"

"I don't know. I guess it just felt like more than working off the rush that came from getting us through it. It's all right, Drummond."

He stood and walked toward her. No, not walked, stalked across the room like some large, predatory beast. "Did you miss the part where I told you I threw away the key to your collar, Blaise? I'll admit that a couple of times when I was fucking you, it was pure, raw lust fueled by what happened, but not the rest of the time and sure as hell not the first time. That meant something to me. It felt like I'd finally found that missing piece to my soul."

She blinked several times. She'd struck a chord;

she'd actually wounded him. Yesterday morning she might have rejoiced in that and felt smug, now all she felt was ashamed.

"I'm sorry, Gavan. When you said what you did about working off the adrenaline..."

"I meant it, but that wasn't all of it. That wasn't even half of it," he said as he stood next to the bed. "Get rid of the covers. I want to see you naked."

Blaise could feel the corners of her mouth lifting. She was going to have to make her harsh words up to him. Tossing back the bedclothes, she rolled to her knees, lifted her face to his, and wrapped her arms around his strong neck. She rubbed her body against his half-naked, chiseled and muscular torso.

"Kiss me, Master, and please accept my most sincere apologies."

"I do, but you're going to have to do better than that," he said, his voice deepening with lust.

"If you'll let me, I intend to."

"Proceed."

She pulled his sweatpants down, taking care not to touch his rigid member that was so hard that it almost touched his navel. After licking her lips, she then wrapped them around the head of his cock as she wrapped her hand around the shaft. She swirled her tongue, forcing a groan from him. Oh, he might be her Master, but Blaise meant to give as good as she got.

Gavan's hands sank into her red hair, giving it a

tug and lighting up her scalp. He grasped the silky tresses, holding her head in place as he began to thrust. He drove his cock deep, hitting the soft place at the back of her throat. She swallowed him down as she held herself steady with one hand and cupped and stroked the heavy globes hanging behind his cock.

She lifted her head ever so slightly, looking up only to lock eyes with him while he watched his dick moving in and out of her mouth. As he pulled himself back, she sucked frantically trying to keep him inside as her tongue continued its seductive assault over his silky skin. He let his cock slide over her tongue until only his cockhead still had her lips wrapped around him before driving his hips forward, shoving his cock as deep as it would go, his balls slapping her chin.

He lost the measured rhythm of his thrusting as his cock became swollen and twitched just before he erupted into the back of her throat, sending his cum into her belly.

He slid himself free, then pulled his sweatpants back up. "The next time you think to turn that bratty mouth on me, I'll but a ball gag in it and spank your pretty bottom to a deep shade of crimson. If you don't understand something, or if something I say isn't clear, or you have questions, you talk to me. Clear?"

"Yes, Master. I'm so very sorry."

He chuckled. "You're going to pay for it, *brèagha*. You take those pretty tits with their stiff nipples and what I'm sure is a very ripe and ready pussy and go take a cold shower. Nothing for you until tonight."

"Gavan..."

"That's right, Gavan, Master, or Sir. The next time you call me *Drummond* in that derisive tone, you'll take five hard."

Her entire body shook with need. Not only was she aroused because it was morning and he had yet to fuck her, but giving head always did that to her and Gavan had a way of making her half-crazy with lust.

"This is just a guess here, but that contract is going to say no masturbating, isn't it?"

"I don't think that's how I'd put it, more that all your sexual stimulation, pleasure, and satisfaction will come from me."

She groaned. "Are you allowed to masturbate?"

"Allowed? Yes, but why would I when I have such a sweet fuck toy to play with?"

She felt herself blush, but wasn't sure if it was embarrassment, annoyance, or pride, probably a bit of all three.

He helped her off the bed and got dressed while she took a miserably cold shower that only seemed to alleviate the tiniest bit of her need. Once she was out of the bathroom, he sat in the wingback chair and watched her dress.

"Do you want me to have them send something up, join the clan downstairs, or wait and eat with Vera?"

"Would your people be terribly hurt if we joined Vera? I almost feel bad about leaving her yesterday, but I know she had your guys, and I can't regret anything that led to last night," she said, pulling on her boots. Vera had packed her a pair of black denim leggings, along with a slouchy black knit tunic and an outrageously sexy lace bra.

Gavan stood and walked over to her, lowering his face until they touched foreheads. "And with that admission, I forgive you for your earlier faux pas."

"I thought that's what the blow job was for."

He shook his head. "No way. I get blow jobs on demand. You want to atone for misbehavior with me, it'll usually take getting spanked and apologizing, but I decided to be magnanimous this morning."

She laughed out loud, then rolled her eyes. "You're just too good to me, Master."

"Yes," he said. "Yes, I am."

He brought her hand up to his lips, kissing her fingers before leading her out of the bedroom, down the stairs, and out to the waiting helicopter.

"Are you okay with the chopper?" he asked solicitously.

"Not totally, but I want to be. And I trust you to keep me safe."

Twenty minutes later, the helicopter, which carried her and Gavan, as well as four security guards who relieved the compound and field patrols, landed at Kilted Fire. The pilot would take these four back, then return for Gavan and the two men in the house.

"We'll need to put in a helipad," he said with a grin. He'd noted halfway through the chopper ride that she'd relaxed and enjoyed it.

"That's on your dime, laddie."

He shook his head. "Behave yourself, *brèagha*. Vera's seen a sub disciplined before. It won't bother her in the least."

Ducking below the rotors, she and Gavan left the helicopter and headed into the house. They'd brought a breakfast basket Nessa had sent with them that had crepes, scotch eggs, a frittata, muffins, and shakshuka, something Gavan loved. It sounded disgusting to her for breakfast, but she decided she'd give it a try.

As they laid all the food out on the table, Vera said, "Apparently your Nessa doesn't believe in anyone going hungry."

Gavan laughed as the security personnel dug in. "No, she just knows the boys. Blaise, you need something more substantial than a blueberry muffin."

"I thought you took care of that earlier when you came down my throat," she said, innocently sipping her tea.

Gavan damn near spit the hot liquid in his mouth back into his mug; and the men eating with them stopped their forks midway to their mouths.

"Careful, *brèagha*. I doubt very much the boys would mind seeing you get spanked."

She grinned at him. "Any chance I can get away with mouthing off at you?"

"Sweetheart, you can do whatever you like…"

"Don't believe him, Blaise. That's what Doms say when they want to get their hands on your ass and leave a mark," said Vera.

"Yes. I'm figuring that out."

"She doesn't need any encouragement from you, McDonald. And as for you, *brèagha*, you might want to keep in mind that Doms can get a vicarious thrill from watching another Dom deal with his or her sub."

Blaise shook her head. After they'd eaten and as Gavan was getting ready to leave, he pulled both she and Vera aside. "No kidding. I don't want either of you to go anywhere by yourself."

"It's broad daylight and it's the distillery," argued Vera.

"Where somebody already set a fire and most likely dispatched a goon squad. My sub will bloody well do what I say or face the consequences of her actions. As for you, Mistress Vera, I can haul your skinny ass up to my castle and no one will come to save you. By the way, the celebration of Lachlan's life at the club is tomorrow night."

"Gavan said we could do a collaring ceremony if I wanted, and I think my grandfather would have liked that."

Vera's eyes glistened with tears. "I think it would be fitting and make him very happy."

"There's only one problem. My master tells me there was only one key and he tossed it away." Blaise turned to Gavan. "If you think I'm letting you cut my collar off, you're wrong."

"We'll just present it as a fait accompli and tell them why."

Not only was Blaise surprised that he would admit such a romantic gesture at his own club, but she was also strangely touched by it. She walked out with him to the waiting helicopter with her new bodyguard trailing behind her.

"Seriously, even out to the helicopter?"

"He'll never be more than two steps behind or in front of you, except when you go in the loo, and you'd best be quick about that because he won't give you more than five minutes before he comes busting in. I don't have to tell you how I'll respond if you decide to get cute and play games, do I?"

"No, Master. I'll behave. But I am getting laid tonight, right?

Gavan placed his hand over the hard bulge in his trousers. "What do you think?"

"Then I will be on my very best behavior," she purred, running her tongue along his bottom lip before kissing him deeply.

She turned and ducked under the rotating blades as they started up and Gavan got into the helicopter.

"You're going to be a pain in the ass, aren't you?"

her security guard asked without rancor once they were near the house.

"Probably, but not today."

She waved to Gavan and blew him a kiss, seriously wondering how she was going to get through the day without him.

CHAPTER 18

*H*amish was waiting for him when the helicopter returned to Castle Cat-Sith. Once at the main keep, Gavan entered and exchanged greetings and pleasantries with his people. He ventured back to the kitchen and waited until Nessa looked to be at a good stopping point.

"Gavan? Was there something amiss?" she asked.

"Never. The food was excellent. I'd like your help in finding someone for Kilted Fire. Vera McDonald will be staying there, so I don't think a whole staff will be needed or welcomed."

"I'll start looking. Does it have to be human?"

"I don't think so."

"Will the Teine be held this weekend? I only ask because of your lady not being one of us yet and thinking about what I need to plan for."

"I won't cancel the Teine, but I'm not certain if

my mate and I will be in attendance or not. I'm going to be fairly busy for the next few days, so if you could coordinate with Hamish on what you might need, I'd appreciate it."

Blushing, she said, "Of course, Gavan. Thank you."

Hamish followed him out and back to Gavan's study. He flipped through the messages and paperwork on his desk.

"You don't need to do that," said Hamish quietly.

"Don't I? You've been telling me since she got here that you didn't feel you could take a mate until I did. Now that I have, it's your turn."

"You've got more important things to think about than my love life."

"Maybe, but aside from Blaise, nothing that is as much fun." Gavan sat in the office chair behind his desk. "What do we know?" he asked his second in command.

"I'm fairly convinced it isn't any of the other syndicate leaders."

"I can almost guarantee that. When we split up so I could shift, they went after Blaise."

"Doesn't completely rule it out. Word has spread like wildfire that you have a woman."

"I want someone with her and Vera at all times until I'm sure we have everything secured. Put the word out that I will destroy anything and anyone who harms either of them."

"Not to be nosy, but why are you protecting a retired cop?"

"Because I gave Lachlan Munro my word that I would. He died trusting me to hold to that. She'd be safer if she was up here, but as you point out, she's a retired cop and a smart one. We don't need her poking around up here."

"You need to tell her, Gavan."

"Vera?" he said, confused.

"No. Blaise. She needs to know. She has a right to know. Besides, the ability to shift and shred someone with her claws or crush their skulls in her jaws might come in handy."

"I know." Gavan sighed. "Things have been moving a lot faster than I ever thought they would. Part of me wants to damn Lachlan for putting us in this situation, but part of me knows I owe the old bastard big time."

Hamish grinned. "You do seem rather settled with her, and the change in you is already being noticed. People will be glad to hear that the Teine will be held as usual, though there will still be some speculation."

"What's the betting pool look like?" Gavan asked with a wry grin.

"Some think you'll keep her away and wait until the next one to bring her; others are betting you'll turn her and bring her this time. There are a few who think you'll cancel, but that's only a tiny minority.

Care to share your thoughts so I can make the appropriate bet?"

"Originally, I thought to keep her away, but then I never thought she'd greet me naked and on her knees last night. Your point about her having the right to know is well founded."

"I'm happy for you, Gav. She's tough and strong and I believe she suits you to a tee. She will make a magnificent tigress."

Gavan nodded. Hamish had valuable insight. The ability to shift into a tigress would give Blaise a leg up in any situation.

"I've got a few calls I want to make. Do you need anything else from me?"

"No. I think that covers it." Hamish started to leave but stopped at the door. "There is one thing. The fire chief is making a lot of noise about being kept from doing a proper investigation into what happened at Kilted Fire."

"Fuck. We don't know what happened other than it looks like sabotage. Any new information on any of the distillery's competitors?"

"The big single malt distillers are talking about trying to get her license revoked because of your involvement. They don't like the idea of the syndicate moving into their business."

"Moving in? Who do these bastards think they are on their high horses? Most of them have taken loans from criminal organizations because the banks deem them as too risky. And some are laundering money for various syndicates. Besides, we can ensure that doesn't happen. But what's interesting is what's got a bug up the chief's bum? He's usually pretty easy to deal with and he owes us. Gently remind him of that for me."

"And on a happier note," Hamish said, trying to lighten the darkness that had clouded Gavan's expression. "The club called and wanted to ensure the celebration for Lachlan was still on for tomorrow."

"It is. I'm going to take Blaise into Inverness tomorrow and see if she won't let me spoil her."

"Now how would you spoil a woman like Blaise? She doesn't wear much jewelry, though she did seem to like her collar. She kept touching it, but not like she wanted to be rid of it. I just can't see her valuing a lot of things that seem to interest other women."

Gavan laughed. "No, she'd be impressed by another still or kiln. But I did talk her into letting me replace that piece of shit truck she has. Only it turns out it was her granda's first vehicle and he taught her to drive in it before giving it to her. So, while we're in Inverness tomorrow ordering her new Range Rover, haul the truck off but see if we can't find someone who can restore and fix it for her."

"Before I forget, the PR firm would like some of your time. Do you want to do a conference call or maybe meet with them tomorrow while you're in Inverness?"

"The latter I think. Have them look at Kilted

Fire's marketing and tell them I'd like a broad outline of what they can do to boost sales. I told Blaise she's going to need to hire some help and that I want a business plan by the end of the week."

Hamish nodded. "Good enough. Do you plan to stay in Inverness?"

"As much as I'd like to, I think we're safer back here on Skye. Make sure the distillery has enough security to ensure that Vera is protected as well. She'll need transportation to and from the event. I'll make sure she's on board with that. I don't know that whoever came after Blaise is interested in her personally or in harming Kilted Fire."

"We'll take care of it. Any chance I can send a couple of our men with you and Blaise?"

"No. I don't want her spooked but let's up the security at the club."

"Done."

After Hamish left, Gavan spent the next several hours working through phone calls, finalizing plans for Lachlan's celebration and convincing the caterers that they could manage a small tiered and decorated cake for his and Blaise's collaring ceremony. He saved his favorite phone call for last.

"Blaise Munro," she answered.

"Hello, my sweet and beautiful sub."

"Hello, my Master," she purred. "How is your day going?"

"Since I left you, it's been rather dreary. I thought

we'd spend the day in Inverness tomorrow. We have an appointment to meet with the people who do my marketing. I'd like them to take a look at what you're doing for Kilted Fire. I think the lack of advertising is holding you back."

"It's not just advertising, it's capacity. We can't meet a higher demand. I want to put together two business plans for you. One that I'd been working on and one with more of an investment on your part."

"Scratch the first one. Regardless of your decision at the end of the year, I want to see you and Kilted Fire soar."

"What decision?"

"The one where you decide to terminate our contract and buy back your company," he said softly.

"I wasn't aware the two were mutually exclusive."

Gavan's day brightened considerably. "No, I don't suppose they are. Do you have any of your club wear with you? I know a lot of subs at Baker Street have assigned lockers."

"Yes, and most of my things are there. I could get one of the girls to overnight me something. Oh wait, I now have a Dom."

"I would have thought that point had been brought home to you yesterday."

"No, silly." He doubted anyone had ever called him silly before. "The next time you're going to London, could we visit Dark Garden? Everything I've seen from there is gorgeous, but he will only sell to Doms."

He laughed. "You really are my kind of girl. Range Rovers and expensive corsets. And I wish you'd said something earlier because we could have gone today."

"He rarely has anything off the shelf, so-to-speak, so I doubt it would have mattered."

"Maybe he can make an exception…"

"Gavan, it isn't necessary."

"I'm not so sure of that. I find myself sitting here not liking the idea of you wearing a corset in which you served another Dom at our collaring ceremony."

"I scened and played with others. You are the only man I have ever called Master or served. And it's been so long since I've been to Baker Street that I almost forgot about the corset I ordered and had sent here, so I will have something new for our ceremony."

"After the meeting with the advertising people, I thought we'd go order your new Range Rover."

"You don't have to buy me or Kilted Fire a new SUV," she protested.

"But I do, and if twisting your arm last night didn't convince you, my guess is a trip over my knee will. What do you think?"

"I think the arm twisting will suffice."

"I thought it might," he chuckled. "Can you be ready at five?"

"If you want me to pack for Inverness, can it be

six? I told the boys that they could get the stills set for the night, and I'd just check them before I leave."

"Six it is, and Blaise, why don't you pack a large bag and bring some more of your things?"

He ended the call and stared at it for a moment as a slow smile began to spread across his face. So, she didn't think the two were mutually exclusive. He could live with that. If she wanted, he'd give her his share of the company as a wedding present. It sounded as if Blaise could see a future with him and that would make all the difference.

CHAPTER 19

When Gavan ended the call, she kept the phone in her hand and gazed out the window. He was something of an enigma. Yet, in some ways, he was so transparent: deceptively simple but deeply complex. And she was falling for him. She quickly remembered how Tommy had warned her off Gavan only this morning.

"I can't believe you're fucking Gavan Drummond."

"And I can't believe you'd say that to me. What's the matter, Tommy? You jealous? You're not his type."

She was irrationally angry at Tommy. Granted, he shouldn't have shared what she'd told him with his boyfriend, Craig, but Tommy hadn't necessarily known that Craig would blab to the chief. But added to that was the fact that Tommy had tried to usurp her authority and get by her to Gavan. Luckily for her, Gavan preferred pussy over everything else.

"I was out of line yesterday, Blaise. You jumped down my throat about Craig. In retrospect, I shouldn't have told him, but I never thought he'd go to his boss. I guess I just didn't want him to think I was a total screw-up."

"So, then what's your problem with Gavan?"

"He's a gangster," said Tommy. "I mean, he's the head of the Galloglass Syndicate. You don't even know the guy."

"I've lived on Skye for more than a decade. You don't live here more than six months and not know who he is. I also know he owns Termonn in Inverness. It's a lifestyle club like the one I belong to in London."

"Lifestyle club—you mean a BDSM club?" She nodded, trying hard not to laugh at his disapproving look. "Why didn't you join his club?"

Blaise laughed. "Because my granda, I think, was one of the founding members at Termonn and I thought it would be too weird. That really isn't important. What is important is that I do know who Gavan Drummond is and I am going into this with my eyes wide open."

"What is *this*?"

"Honestly, that doesn't concern you. What should concern you is that if you ever try an end-run play around me again, I'll fire you on the spot. Gavan has left all day-to-day operations to me, and as I said, you're not his type."

"Do you want me to resign?" Tommy asked, seeming to hold his breath.

"Not necessary. Just don't do it again. Look, Tommy. Gavan has money he's willing to invest in Kilted Fire. Some of the things I only ever dreamed of doing might be possible. We're meeting at his marketing firm tomorrow."

Tommy shook his head. "Are you really throwing another celebration of life for your grandfather at a kink club?" he asked, his voice dripping with disapproval.

"As a matter of fact, I am. D/s was an important part of my granda's life, and he has friends there who wouldn't have felt any more comfortable coming here than you feel about going there. Gavan and I are going to leave in the morning. We'll stop by here first and be home tomorrow night."

"And are you calling that castle of his home?"

"For now," she said non-committally. "I don't know about you, but I have a lot to do if I'm going to be gone tomorrow. I'm heading up to the house to see if I can make any sense out of the books."

Tommy had a point. Gavan was a gangster. He didn't even bother trying to hide it and she questioned, thrown away key notwithstanding, whether or not he thought they had much of a future beyond a year. Maybe he was right. Blaise wasn't sure if he even wanted a future together or that she did, but she hadn't liked the fact that it seemed like he'd assumed they didn't.

As she'd told Tommy, she knew who and what he was. She wondered if that might change or if he was as bad as some people said. Many people were scared to death of him, and rightfully so. She walked through all the buildings on her way up to the house. Her grandfather had always said it was important for the workers to see the boss, whoever it might be, every day.

By the time she got to the kitchen, Vera was fixing lunch.

"I thought you might be headed up this way. I made enough for two. Nothing fancy, but it'll fill a hole in your belly. Although, after that little discussion at breakfast, it sounds like Lord Drummond may be taking care of that for you."

Blaise laughed. "I want to grow up to be you."

"A wrinkled old Domme with nothing but memories to keep her warm?"

Blaise ran to embrace her as a shadow of grief passed over her eyes. They filled their plates with the lamb stew Vera had made and tore off chunks of crusty artisan bread before going to the kitchen table and sitting down.

"Only if that's what you want. You need to know Granda would have been the first to tell you to find someone else you can be happy with, and I'd second that. Regardless of what you decided about that, I really would love it if you'd consider this place your home and stay. And what I meant was a strong woman who speaks her mind and doesn't give a shit about what people think."

"Your granda helped me with that." She shook her head, smiling from a memory. "We didn't start out as Domme and sub. Initially, he was the Dom and I was his sub because that's the way we thought it should be. He talked a lot to Gavan, and it was Gavan who made him see that it didn't have to be that way and that we should be whoever we wanted to be. Did you know that Gavan was my mentor at the club? The Doms and Dommes have mentors; the subs have trainers."

"Was he really?" And she couldn't help the dazed expression that filtered over her features as she pictured Gavan at the club.

She nodded. "You're falling for him, aren't you?"

"Yes, and that worries me. I've known him for years and been about half in love with him for just as long. He's a curious man. One minute I think I know him and the next, he's a total mystery."

"That would be the very definition of Gavan Drummond, a puzzle wrapped in a mystery bound in an enigma. There are a lot of people on both sides of the law who are afraid of him, and rightfully so. He can be a ruthless sonofabitch."

"But you like him…"

"And respect him. He can kill a man without thinking twice about it, but never an innocent. I've never known him to take out anyone who didn't deserve it. He'll kill a pimp that hurts a hooker in the blink of an eye, then help that hooker get out of the business. Gavan and his compatriots—Con O'Neill in Ireland, Joshua Knight in England and Braden Hughes in Wales—seem to have some kind of loose collective where they take on the really bad guys: the Bratva, the Cartels, and the like. Your Gavan has a code of honor and I've never known him to break it. As far as I know, he's never, ever, harmed a woman."

"Do you think he'd give up his criminal businesses?"

Vera leaned back in her chair. "Now, that's a very interesting question; I'm not sure I know the answer to that, but I will say that for the most part, he's the master of the victimless crimes. The hookers who work for him want to. He doesn't traffic or force women in any way. They'd take their stiletto heels to you if you tried to harm him. He's one of the best smugglers in the world. Some of what he smuggles is his, but some is for others. He has muscle for hire, but not assassins. Like I said, an interesting man. Do you think you could live with it if he wouldn't?"

"I'm ashamed to say maybe. I'd want to know what every single thing was and if he's the man you and my grandfather described, then definitely maybe. I know there's a connection with him I've never felt before, not just the sex or the spankings, but something far deeper."

"Then that, my girl, is worth exploring and fighting for if you have to. Your collar, by the way, is gorgeous."

She nodded and touched it absent-mindedly. "I've never seen anything like it."

"My guess is that he had it made for you."

"So, he did know about the will."

Vera shook her head. "No, at least not before the last time he met with your grandfather. Your grandfather had prepared the will before he talked to Gavan. There's no way he could have had that made in that short amount of time."

"Then he probably had it made for someone else or no one at all."

"I wouldn't say that to him. My guess is he'd decided you were the woman he wanted and was making plans for that to happen."

"Maybe. He did tell me that the will had only given him leverage."

"See? You need to think about how you deal with Gavan. He's run a large criminal organization for more than fifteen years, and he's never been arrested. He's been taken in for questioning, but never has he been charged with a crime. He's a strategic thinker and usually has a plan in place plus a contingency plan ready to go before he ever makes a move. But all that aside, Blaise. Does he make you happy?"

"We haven't been together that long. How would I know?"

"There are no time limitations on happiness. Your grandfather always said that he thought you spent far too much time thinking. My observation says that's a common trait among subs. They get inside their own heads and can't get out. That's why they need a Dom, someone who can keep them grounded, keep them in the here and now. You can't think this one through, Blaise. You just have to feel it. Are you happy when you're with Gavan?"

"Yes, when you put it like that. You know about what happened last night, right?"

"With the gunmen? Yes."

"I was more afraid to get on Gavan's helicopter than I was when they were trying to kill us. I knew— deep down in my bones—that Gavan would take care of me. That he would die before he'd let anything hurt me. I think it shocked the shit out of him that the gunmen came after me and not him."

"What do you mean?" asked Vera with renewed interest.

"After they forced us off the road, Gavan got me out of the Range Rover and sent me away, ostensibly to go back to the road to get help. What he thought is they were after him and he wanted to draw them away. When they followed me instead, Gavan came after them and between his men and himself, they got all of them."

Vera smiled. "You do know that the incident wasn't reported and none of those men were turned over to the authorities."

"Do you think they're dead? That Gavan killed them?"

"Unless they can tell him something with enough value that offsets that they tried to harm you, probably so. You need to think about the fact that he's now vulnerable because of his feelings for you. Remember when you think to defy him, that there might be more at stake than you can see. You make him share with you and when he orders you to stay put or to go with one of his men, you do it."

Blaise heard her wise words, but opted to change the subject. "Gavan and I are taking the helicopter into Inverness in the morning. I have to stop by here anyway. Do you want to come along? We have a couple of meetings..."

"I love helicopters! Yes, I won't be a third wheel. You two go do whatever you need to do. I've got friends I can see and if you really want me out here, I think I'll call one who's an estate agent to list my flat."

"I'm so glad. You should move into the master bedroom. It's kind of old and really masculine so if and when you decide to fix it up, I can help if you like."

"That should be your room. I can take the gatekeeper's cottage."

"If you like, but I'd really like it if you moved in up here, unless it would bother you."

"No, sweetie, I have nothing but the best memories of this place. I wouldn't trade any of the time I had with your grandfather, even the last few weeks. Besides, this big ole house shouldn't be empty, and I think you'll be up at the castle."

They chatted for a while more until Blaise set off to review the distillery's books. When the helicopter landed that evening, Blaise was waiting with a large, packed bag. She had a moment of concern when Gavan exited the chopper and spied the size of the bag that maybe she'd overstepped.

He grasped the handle of the suitcase and leaned down to brush his lips against hers. "You should have packed a bigger bag... or maybe two."

CHAPTER 20

Gavan hoped she'd decided to stay, because he was never going to let her go. Her body and spirit called not only to his human self, but to his altered self as well. It had taken every bit of his iron control not to pull her to her knees, take the nape of her neck and bite down, initiating the Gift.

He tried to tell himself that he wanted to turn her for her own protection and while that was certainly in the column of why he should do it, the bigger reason was that he wanted her to become one with him. He didn't want any secrets between them, and he desperately wanted to sink his cock deep inside her and loosen his barbs so that each time he drew back, they would score her most tender flesh. He wanted her to yowl as he stroked her over and over.

Even so, they'd taken each other to dizzying heights the night before. Blaise was easy to arouse, but quick to become frustrated and act out, which led him to justifying forced orgasm after forced orgasm from her. There was something about watching her writhe and struggle, sometimes trying to get away, other times clinging to him as if she couldn't get close enough.

She lay sleeping beside him with her red hair splayed all over the pillow. He nuzzled her neck and rumbled low in his throat to her. Even though she'd yet to be turned, she was already beginning to respond when he made the chuffing sound to her. Her body was resplendently naked and outrageously curvy. Blaise had teased him that her tits were more than a mouthful and he reminded her that he had a large appetite.

She was absolutely gorgeous but what called to him the most was the strength of her character and the resiliency of her spirit. Every now and again, he could see her grief, but instead of wallowing in it, she acknowledged it and moved on. He could see the evidence of his use all over her body from the swollen lips from his kisses to the beard burn on the inside of her thighs. All and all, she had the appearance of a woman who had been fucked hard, long, and repeatedly, and had rejoiced in every minute.

Slowly, her great green eyes opened. He guessed that they would be startling and beautiful when she was a black tigress. Normally, purebred tigers had yellow eyes with dark irises, except for white tigers which had blue eyes, but shifters' eyes often retained the color of their human selves.

"What are you thinking about?" she asked softly.

"I'm thinking about how I should have made a move on you long before now."

"What makes you think you would have been successful?"

He traced his index finger from the top of her mons down over her clit, following the natural path to her pussy before penetrating her by curling his finger up and stroking. Blaise arched her back and her hands caught his wrists, not to try and pull his hand away but to give her something to clench as her body trembled.

"Just a wild guess," he teased. He wanted them just to be able to go on as they were, but he knew it wasn't possible and the longer he wasn't completely honest with her, the more he risked losing her all together.

"What's with the furrowed brow?" she said, reaching up to soothe it.

"There are things you need to know about me…"

"I know you're a gangster, Gavan. That's not exactly a secret. Before you worry yourself into a tizzy…"

"Doms don't do tizzies."

"Well before you upset yourself in whatever ways alpha males do to deal with things."

"Mostly they spank the hell out of their bratty subs."

She laughed. His woman was not the least bit afraid of him, and if all he had to tell her was that he was a gangster, they'd be home free, but it wasn't. Even though she wore his collar, he felt the need to tell her the truth so that she could make an informed decision. He'd had breakfast brought up to their room and she crawled into his lap so he could feed her. He knew he needed to share her with his clan at meals, but for right now, he was selfish and wanted her all to himself, especially if she decided she couldn't accept who and what he was.

"Just answer me this: did you ever kill anyone who didn't deserve to die?"

"No," he said, shaking his head.

"Did you ever deal drugs or force a woman into prostitution?"

Clearly, Vera had been talking to her. "Never."

"Did you ever do something that might be considered treason?"

"Definitely not."

"Then we can work through the rest. I won't tell you that I'm comfortable knowing you break the law as a way to make a living, but there are very few people on Skye who don't speak well of you. I can even wrap my head around the fact that you probably killed or will kill those men who tried to kill us. God help me, but I can't see anything wrong in that. Hell,

Vera used to be a cop and even she told me that you lived by a code of honor. However, I do want to meet your three friends."

"And you will. I wish all you had to contend with was that I run the Galloglass Syndicate."

He stood, putting distance between them and shoving the bolt home in the enormous bedroom door's lock. There was no way to ease into this, no way to lead up to what he had to tell her. The one thing he wasn't worried about was her divulging the true nature of him and his clan. Betrayal wasn't any part of her DNA.

She sat up in their bed, drawing her knees up close to her chest. "Gavan, what is it?"

"How much do you know about evolution?"

"Probably a bit more than most people. I found it an interesting subject in college."

"What if I were to tell you that back before the beginning of recorded time, a powerful sorceress gifted four of her familiars—those she thought were the strongest and bravest—with the ability to shift from their beast to their human selves and that their descendants developed along a parallel path to that of humans."

"I'd think you'd been drinking the good scotch and not saving any for me," she said, laughing.

"I know it sounds fantastical, but it's true."

"Seriously, Gavan, are you feeling okay?" she said,

rising from the bed like the goddess in the *Birth of Venus* and coming to lay her hand on his forehead.

Like a magnet pointing true north, his dick rose immediately to the occasion. Where Blaise Munro was concerned, his cock had the worst sense of timing, no sense of decorum and a one-track mind. *Down boy*.

Pussy!

Blaise glanced down between them. "Well, at least we know that part's working. I was a little concerned that we might have broken it last night."

He chuckled. "No, baby. As far as you're concerned, my dick is the fucking *Energizer Bunny*. It doesn't matter how hard or how long you use it, it's always ready to burrow back into that sweet pussy of yours." Gavan took his hands in hers. He couldn't tell if she didn't sense the seriousness of their discussion or did and was trying to deflect it. In either case, it wasn't going to work. "You have to believe me."

She tried to pull away, but he held fast. "That's ridiculous, Gavan. Nobody can change into some kind of half-man, half-beast. "

"Not half and half, at least not at the same time, but a completely unique creature that can shift between two beings, one human and one animal."

"You want me to believe werewolves are real?"

"If you mean the kind you see in *Harry Potter* or other fantasy films, no. We're not some kind of tortured, misshapen creature whose form is dictated by the moon. The goddess gave my kind the ability to shape-shift from man to beast at will."

"And what kind of beast are you? Satyr? I mean that would make sense, you can fuck all night long and you're certainly well-endowed."

Her mind was searching for some kind of rational explanation other than the truth.

"You need to know that you are as safe with my altered self as you are standing here with me now. Maybe safer. He can't spank your pretty ass when you brat off at him. My mind is unchanged. I retain the ability to think as a man and can remember everything I've ever done, be it as man or beast."

Gavan moved away from her, giving himself room. He closed his eyes and called his black tiger forward. He could feel and see as the shimmer surrounded him, causing the room and her to go soft focus for only a moment until his eyes changed and once more the black tiger could see with keen eyesight.

He expected her to scream, to try to get away, to draw back, to collapse into a dead faint, but Blaise did none of the above. Her eyes widened and the pulse in her neck beat more strongly, but she wasn't afraid.

Putting her hand out, she walked slowly toward him. "Gavan? If this is a joke, it's not funny."

Closing the distance between them, he rubbed his long, furred body against her legs, making a noise that was as close to a purr as his tiger vocal cords could do.

"Gavan?" she said again. "My grandfather knew, didn't he?"

Gavan continued to rub against her, allowing his thick silky coat to brush along her naked flesh. She took a few steps back and sat down on the mattress. "Really?" she asked.

He made the chuffing noise again as he sprang onto the bed and wrapped his body all around her. Laying his head in her lap, he tickled her nose with his tail. Even though she wasn't aroused at the moment, he could still smell himself on her and traces of her arousal from the night before remained. He sniffed at her sex, rumbling low and seductively.

"Oh, hell to the no," she said, jumping up. "You change back right now."

He did so and she was confronted by the same man who'd fucked her so thoroughly the night before and whose cock really had no sense of decorum and wanted to fuck her again.

"Can you do it again?"

He smiled and called forth the tiger, who once again chuffed to her and rubbed up against her, lifting his head to rub it on her belly before drawing away and shifting back.

"Let me grab a pair of jeans," he said, picking them up from the floor, pulling them on, and stuffing his unruly cock inside the fly as he buttoned them up. "Before you go there, no I have no desire to fuck you as a tiger. I'm beginning to believe the desire to fuck you is ever present but mating or fucking is only done in human form."

"Holy shit! And swearing when your Dom and lover reveals he's a—what did you call it?"

"Shape-shifter in general. With my kind, a black tiger-shifter."

"Your kind? So, you're not the only? Oh my god, is your clan…"

He nodded. "Black tigers all."

"Are you born like this?"

"We're born as humans with the ability to shift there but somewhat dormant. As a child begins to mature, the animal makes itself known. We're taught to shift and to keep our kind secret. Humans aren't exactly known for their tolerance."

"I would never tell anyone…"

"That thought never entered my mind. And you thought being with a gangster would be the difficult part," he said, starting toward her. He needed to get his hands on her, to reassure her, to reassure himself. "I need to know I haven't lost you."

CHAPTER 21

"*L*ost me?"

He had to be kidding. Was he really so clueless about her feelings for him? They were like those of a storm. But she was no summer storm that blew in and was gone in the blink of an eye. No, her feelings were those of a winter storm: violent, wild, and devastating in its intensity, leaving behind a sense of triumph for having survived it at all.

How could he think that? He was the strongest, most dominant creature she'd ever met. He controlled a gangland syndicate and Vera said he was one of the most feared men in the UK, yet he was worried about losing her? She'd never thought she'd see this more vulnerable side. She'd even decided that she could learn to live with him never being able to be completely transparent and open with her.

Blaise knelt in front of him, taking his hands in

hers and laying her cheek against them before looking at him. "You could never lose me, Master. Never."

He dropped to his knees and wrapped his arms around her. "Thank God. I've never wanted or needed anything or anyone as badly as I do you."

She realized that this was a side he would never show anyone else. Only she would see this version of him. Gavan rolled onto his feet. She understood now why his movements were always so graceful and predatory. He was, in every way, a lethal predator —*her* lethal predator.

"How are your people going to feel about you being with a human?" she asked.

"It isn't unheard of, and they know you. Regardless of their feelings, I am alpha. They will accept my decision."

"Do people usually choose someone within the clan?"

"Sometimes, but we learned long ago to bring in fresh blood and often that's human. But for me, the most important thing is whether or not they belong together. Do they make each other happy? Our kind believes each of us has a fated mate, one person who is born to complete us in every way. You are mine."

She searched his face. There was more. "Tell me."

"I want you to become one with me."

"I don't understand."

"I want you to become a tigress."

"You mean I could shift like you?" The idea was intriguing and disturbing at the same time.

"Yes. You would be an incredible black tigress. You'd be healthier, live longer, be stronger, and all of your senses would be heightened."

"How does that work?"

"A virus is introduced into your system and your wholly human DNA gets altered to that of a black tiger-shifter."

"So, all it takes is a shot?" That seemed way too easy. "How big is the needle? I hate needles."

He started to laugh, then pulled her close. "Not to worry, *brèagha*. No needles are involved."

"Then how?"

"Tigers are very sensual creatures. I will take you from behind and as you climax, my fangs will elongate. Like with most felines when they are mating, I will grasp your neck and bite down."

"That sounds painful."

"I won't lie to you, it is. The pain will be sharp but exquisite. Besides, I'll have you focused on other things. The bite will also allow me to release the barbs that cover my cock."

"Barbs? I've seen your cock. I've had it inside me and gone down on you. As amazing and enormous as it is, it doesn't have barbs," she said with a nervous laugh.

"It does. I've been repressing them. As I thrust in, they'll feel just like an embellishment, but when I draw back, they'll be activated and score your inner walls. I'm told for a tigress there's a bite of pain, but most females find it amplifies their pleasure and they tend to yowl quite loudly, which just encourages your mate to redouble his efforts." He placed his mouth close to her ear. "I will make you scream in so many ways."

Blaise could feel the heat rising. Gavan could overwhelm her senses so easily. What he was suggesting was terrifying, but she felt herself nodding. It didn't matter. She trusted him. The connection between them was profound. It was easy to believe he was right that they were fated to be together and thus why it was so easy to allow herself to submit to him in all ways. It seemed almost impossible to be agreeing to change her life—hell her DNA—and yet there was a peace that only he could provide, and she would give him the same.

"You're saying yes?" he asked, nuzzling her.

"I'm saying I want to be one with you... in all ways."

"Then it's settled. Tonight, you will formally accept my collar."

"And the other?"

"Each month the clan celebrates Oidhche Teine or just Teine on the full moon and it happens to be this weekend. It is then that I will initiate the Gift."

Love, lust, joy, and pride. His emotions swirled all around him. Gavan's greatest fear had been that she would run from him, and he would lose her forever. Instead, she'd given him her trust in the most profound way possible and had agreed to become one with him. Tonight, they would celebrate her grandfather's life with those who'd loved him at the club, and she would formally accept his collar.

As he helped her into the helicopter, he realized something else he loved about her: she embraced each new experience with such unabandoned enthusiasm. Hamish had been right; she would be a magnificent tigress. Gavan leaned into the area behind the cockpit and kissed her hard.

"I forgot my phone. I'll be right back."

He jogged back to the house and up the stairs. He opened the safe in their bedroom, grabbed the ring box, and shoved it deep into the front pocket of his jeans. He rejoined her and the pilot took off, stopping briefly at Kilted Fire to pick up Vera.

Gavan had known Vera for many years. He'd mentored her when she and Lachlan had realized they'd assumed the wrong roles in their relationship, and she'd become a member of the club's governing committee once she'd achieved her master's rights.

"I hope you don't mind picking me up, Gavan. Blaise didn't seem to think you would."

"We're happy to do it. I arranged for a car and driver for you."

"I'm not so old or deep in my grief that I can't drive." Vera didn't try to hide her questioning expression.

"I wasn't suggesting you were."

Vera shook her head. "No. You were just trying to be kind. Thank you."

"My pleasure," he said, leaning back and wrapping his arm around Blaise.

"What are your plans? Maybe we can meet for an early supper before we go to the club," said Blaise.

Both Gavan and Vera smiled. "Sweetheart, Termonn has one of the best up and coming chefs in the UK. We can eat elsewhere if you like, but the food at the club is some of the best in Inverness. In fact, I'm thinking of acquiring the building next to it and opening a restaurant. We can eat in the lounge or in my private office."

"I think that sounds like an excellent plan."

"You can just return the car here at any time. We're going to the Range Rover dealership, and they're sending a car for us. They'll probably have to order it, but they offered to loan us a vehicle for the day."

The liveried chauffeur opened the door into the spacious passenger compartment of a vintage Rolls Royce.

"Fancy," Blaise teased him as she slid inside. Once they were on their way, she turned to him. "Vera's driver isn't really a driver, is he?"

"No, he isn't. That hit squad was after you. They might be after Vera as well and I promised Lachlan I'd look after you both. Have you thought about what kind of Range Rover you want?"

She shook her head. "Nice change of subject, but I'll let it go for now. And yes, I think I want a red Evoque."

Gavan rolled his eyes. "Nothing like telling someone who might want to harm you 'here I am!'"

She shrugged her shoulders. "What can I say? I like red."

He couldn't have asked for a better day. The only argument they had was over Blaise's new vehicle, mostly because he'd delighted in letting the dealer talk her into what he was sure to be the most expensive Evoque ever made. When Gavan mentioned bullet-proof glass, Blaise had balked, but he'd insisted. Well, he'd done more than insisted.

"You're being over the top."

"No, Blaise, I'm not. The bullet-proof glass is non-negotiable." When she'd folded her arms and refused to speak, he wisely decided that chuckling at her adorable pout would most likely not resolve the issue. Instead, he said, "Should I start keeping a tally for when we get to the club?"

She looked at him with confusion until his scowl had reminded her who was Dom and who was not. "No, Gavan. That won't be necessary."

He leaned over and kissed her temple before nuzzling her neck and whispering, "See that it isn't."

The celebration of Lachlan's life had been precisely what he'd wanted. People had laughed too hard, drank too much, and thoroughly enjoyed themselves. Finally, when Gavan had stood and asked for the attention of those who were gathered, people had looked at him expectantly. The fact that Lachlan's granddaughter was wearing an exquisite collar and had never been far from Gavan's side had not gone unnoticed.

"Many of you in this room have been a part of this club since its inception and knew Lachlan quite well. If you did, then you may have surmised who the beauty at my side is. If you didn't, what the hell are you doing at Lachlan's wake?"

There had been a tremor of gentle laughter. Gavan looked down at Blaise, whose dark aubergine corset with black lace trim was stunning. She'd originally had black leather boy shorts to go with it, but Gavan had insisted on a thong and had called a high end fet wear shop to find one that would coordinate.

"Before he died, the old bastard—my apologies Mistress Vera—finally relented and gave me his blessing to claim my beautiful Blaise. She has done me the great honor of agreeing to accept my collar, and now, in front of our friends..." he pulled the ring from the pocket of the black leather vest he had on and dropped to one knee, "...I'd like to ask her if she would grant me my heart's desire and agree to be my wife."

He held up the ring made in the design of and with stones matching her collar: black Cairngorm crystal and white diamonds set in an elaborate, fili-greed, sterling silver setting. He knew people were clapping and urging her to say yes, but in that moment, it seemed that the world had collapsed to just the two of them.

Eyes, sparkling, Blaise nodded.

"Words, *brèagha*. I need to hear you say yes or aye."

"Aye, Gavan. With all that I am, I pledge myself to you."

He was quite sure that the cheer that went up, coupled with all the bartenders popping champagne corks, rattled the windows. Placing the ring on her finger, he kissed her hand and the underside of her wrist before standing and pulling her into his embrace. Her lips had parted easily as he pressed against them with his—his tongue darting in to dance and play with hers. The cheering did not let up until he released her.

Before the commotion died down, Gavan asked her, "Are you all right?"

"Tequila, Master. Tequila."

The rhythmic whooshing of the helicopter's rotor blades had lulled both she and Vera to sleep. The Domme had managed to stay awake when they drove from the club to the helipad, but Blaise had leaned back, rested her head against his shoulder, and promptly fallen asleep as they pulled away from the club. Once they reached the airport, he gathered her in his arms and boarded the helicopter, settling her in the seat beside him. He wasn't sure they'd even cleared Inverness airspace before Vera had joined Blaise in the Land of Nod.

CHAPTER 22

*B*laise didn't remember getting home or being put into bed. The last thing she remembered was Gavan proposing and kissing her repeatedly for the rest of Lachlan's celebration. He'd also become much more physically affectionate, often resting his hand on her ass. While she might have objected anywhere else, in his club, it had seemed right and natural.

She woke as the morning light filtered through the windows. Sensation returned with the breaking of the day. Gavan was a strong and thorough lover and had chosen to celebrate their engagement by fucking her thoroughly and repeatedly. Perhaps she should have objected or resented it, but the fact was that she reveled in his lovemaking, and she now had no doubt that's what it was. His hard body was spooned against hers and his arm was wrapped around her waist with his hand cupping her breast.

Blaise lifted up her hand and looked at her ring. It was stunning. She'd never seen anything like it and was quite sure she'd be happier never knowing how much it cost.

"It doesn't have a lock, *brèagha*, but if it ever comes off your finger, you won't sit down for a week."

She wriggled around so that she was facing him and looped her arms around his neck. Her Master might have fooled the world into thinking he was some kind of all-powerful tiger-shifter, but she knew better. Could he be strict, yes, but for the most part, he was incredibly indulgent.

"Yes, Master," she said before kissing him. "Any chance I can get the helicopter to take me over to Kilted Fire? I have work to do."

He nodded. "Why don't I pick you up and we can join Vera for dinner before we come home."

"You're very sweet, you know that?"

"Shh, *brèagha*. That's a secret between us. We're going to need to get moving. Let's get showered and downstairs. I want to announce to the clan that you've agreed to be my mate before it becomes general knowledge on the island."

"I don't know how to break it to you, but it's a wee bit hard to miss the ring."

Gavan looked at his phone as it vibrated. "Do you

mind getting into the shower alone? I should take this, but…"

"I don't know how to tell you this Drummond, but I've been taking showers by myself long before coming to Skye. The wee lassie is quite capable of bathing herself."

Drummond grinned at her and chose to ignore the phone. "If the wee lassie isn't careful, she's going to get her pretty bottom spanked."

She squealed as he scooped her up in his arms as if he found her weight and her struggling negligible and easily dealt with.

After showering together, Blaise got dressed more quickly than Gavan and headed downstairs to the main dining hall. While she'd known most of his clan from the time she'd come to live on the Isle of Skye, she also knew she needed to make her own place in this new form of family. As she entered the room, Hamish stood up and beckoned her to join him.

His eyes got wide before an enormous smile broke across his face. "I didn't think he'd be so quick to pop the question, but then I didn't think he'd get that collar around your neck so fast either."

"There was no need to delay. We're fated mates."

Dead silence broke across what had been a noisy room. The old saying that she could hear a pin drop seemed apropos.

Hamish held out her chair and she sat down. "Did I say something wrong?"

"So, he told you about our kind?"

"He did."

"Damn the man. I wasn't sure he would. I thought he might get you all wrapped up in being married to him before he shared that with you."

"Do you have any idea how pissed off I'd have been?"

"Yes, and I'm not saying you wouldn't have had the right. To me, and to the clan," Hamish said gesturing to the room, "that he told you first says a lot about how he feels about you. Will you become one with us?"

"Yes. I don't want anything between us. Gavan says there's a celebration this weekend and he'll turn me then."

"Don't be afraid. The claiming bite is painful for a tigress, but the transition is fairly easy and gentle. Wolf-shifters have a hard time of it, and if not managed, it can kill the one being transitioned."

"How awful." She wanted to know more about the barbs but figured Hamish really wasn't the one to ask.

"Let me get you a plate," he offered. "We have breakfast and lunch buffets, and dinner is served family style. Nessa will look to you to make decisions about food and any staff you want to hire here at the castle."

"Is Nessa planning to leave?"

"I hope not, but running of the house will fall to you now and she wouldn't be so bold as to assume..."

"If you see her before I do, tell her to assume away. I'll still be running Kilted Fire, so I'll want all the assistance I can get, but I do want to help Gavan."

"Just having you by his side will do that."

Hamish left her and headed for the huge buffet that lay between a fireplace so big she was certain she could stand in it and a door to what she was sure was the kitchen. She watched him duck into the doorway.

"So," said a lovely brunette with large breasts and too much make-up. Her one single word held visible animosity, enough to make Blaise weary of this conversation.

"Jenna, isn't it?" asked Blaise.

From what she could recall, Jenna worked at the bakery in town. She and Blaise had never been friends, but Blaise had never felt the current venom directed her way before. No doubt Jenna wasn't as happy as Hamish had been about their engagement.

"It is. I don't know why he wants you here."

"Probably because it's easier to fuck me if I'm lying next to him," said Blaise sweetly.

"Ring or not, it'll never last. I set my cap for Gavan a long-time ago and I always get what I want."

Jenna was joined by her long-time partner in nastiness, Eileen. "She's right, you know. You're not even one of us. The others won't stand for it."

"My guess is Gavan won't much care what you

two or anyone else thinks about our being together."

"That's enough, both of you," said Debra, who worked as the teller at the bank.

"It's all right, Debra. They're disappointed. I don't blame them. Never having a chance with Gavan must be devastating for them."

Debra grinned at her. "Trust me, Blaise, neither of them ever had a chance. And you two had better hope our new mistress doesn't share how you treated her with Gavan or Hamish." Turning to Blaise, she continued, "They know better. That's not how this clan greets new members."

"Don't let it concern you, Deb. I've been running Kilted Fire for years. Dealing with disgruntled and nasty people doesn't bother me in the least. Now, the two of you need to stand down or we're going to have trouble."

Eileen's face fell and fear flashed in her eyes. "You'd have Gavan banish us?"

"That would be up to him if he ever heard about this conversation, which he won't from me, but get in my face again and I will personally kick your ass all the way to Inverness."

She recognized the slight shimmer as it began to form around Jenna. *Is this bitch really about to shift and come at me? Bad idea.* Blaise grabbed a steak knife from the table, got Jenna in a headlock and brought the knife up to her throat.

"Really?" she snarled.

"Blaise!" Gavan roared from across the room.

Knowing the danger had passed, Blaise released Jenna, who kept her face averted from Gavan but smiled a wicked, knowing smile. "Gotcha," she whispered as she walked away.

"Are you all right, *brèagha?*" he asked when he'd crossed the room to her side.

"I'm fine, Master," she said, suddenly unsure of herself.

He shook his head. "Master, is it? That means you're buying whatever bullshit Jenna's trying to sell you. That's five you owe me," he said, kissing the tip of her nose before turning toward Jenna who'd almost made it out the door. "Jenna!" he growled.

"Yes, Gavan," she said sweetly.

"Get your ass over here. Eileen, you too."

Blaise wondered how demented she must be to find him incredibly sexy at the moment. There was something about Gavan when he took command that made her heart beat faster, her belly do flip flops, and her pussy do cartwheels.

Both women presented themselves to him. The closer they got, the more their false confidence fled before Gavan's anger.

"Gav," Blaise said, taking her place at his side. "Eileen wasn't the truly nasty one and Debra had my back. And if you'd just waited a few minutes, I could have cut Jenna into little pieces we could dole out to the orcas as snacks."

Gavan looked down at her, obviously fighting the urge to laugh. His eyes crinkled and the corners of his mouth kept trying to lift up. One-by-one, everyone in the room except Gavan, Jenna, and Eileen began to laugh.

"Eileen, you're to stay within the battlement walls for the next week. Jenna, you're allowed out of your room only to go to work for the same amount of time. Your meals will be brought to you and both of you will bloody well apologize to your new mistress."

Eileen couldn't get to her fast enough. Taking Blaise's hand and rubbing her cheek along it, she said "I'm so sorry, Blaise. It will never happen again."

"We're fine, Eileen."

Jenna's body language indicated she was a fool. She was actually thinking of arguing with Gavan. The woman must know nothing about him. That was absolutely the wrong track to take.

"The Teine is this weekend," she whined.

"And you have given up your right to attend. You too, Eileen," Gavan growled. "But if either or both of you are no longer interested in obeying me, you can pack your shit and consider yourselves banished from the castle, if not from the clan."

Both women paled. *Time to soothe the savage beast.*

"Eileen, honey, why don't you go finish your breakfast, then do what you normally do. Jenna? I have no idea why I'm about to stick up for you, but I am. Gavan, she was a complete bitch, but she's always been a bully. She now knows that won't work and I think she realizes what an enormous mistake it would be to continue on this path. Don't you, Jenna?"

Jenna rushed forward and she too rubbed her cheek on Blaise's hand. "My apologies, Blaise. It won't happen again. Ever. Please don't let him toss me out."

"I can't promise anything, but you go up to your room and I'll talk to him. I'll call the bakery to tell them you're feeling under the weather."

"Thank you, Mistress," she said as she scampered from the room.

Blaise turned to the group. "Nothing to see here. Everyone return to what you were doing."

People laughed, applauded, and did just that, including Debra, who squeezed her hand.

"Debra?"

"Yes, Blaise?"

"Don't I remember you took bookkeeping and business courses in college?"

"I did."

"Do you like your job at the bank?"

More laughter.

"I hate it, but it's better since Gavan had the handsy bank manager fired."

"Good. Then give your two-week notice. I can't make any sense of the books my grandfather left me. It's like he wrote them in some kind of code. If you want the job, it's yours. You can ride back and forth with me."

"Oh my God, Blaise. Thank you."

Gavan took her back to her table and held her chair while she sat down. "Well played, *brèagha*. Well played."

Hamish hurried to her side. "I second that and my apologies as well. It shouldn't have happened."

Blaise waived him off with her hand. "It's fine. No harm, no foul."

"I think you both need to go to Kilted Fire," said Hamish, worry creasing his brow.

"Why?"

"Something's gone wrong in the malt barn. Something with the kilns."

Without a further word to anyone, Gavan, Blaise, the pilot and a man who could only be considered some kind of bodyguard, rushed out of the castle to the helicopter where another large, muscled man waited.

"Two?" she asked.

"Be grateful I don't keep you handcuffed to me," he growled.

"Oooh handcuffs. That could be fun," she teased.

Gavan rolled his eyes. "Get in the damn chopper."

"I already did my pre-flight. I left Drew up here to make sure no one messed with it."

Once they were all belted in, the pilot ran a brief double-check, then engaged the engines and lifted off. Fifteen minutes later, they were landing at Kilted Fire.

CHAPTER 23

They'd barely touched ground when Blaise clambered over Drew and rushed to the malt barn.

"It's ruined," Tommy said. "The whole batch is ruined. The malt should have been ready to go in the washbacks."

"What the fuck happened?" she railed.

"It looks like somebody turned up the heat in the kiln. Maybe it was one of Drummond's men, messing around. I told them to stay out of the buildings, but they said it was their job. Maybe it was an accident, but maybe not," said Tommy, who shut up as soon as Gavan joined them.

"Sweetheart?"

"A whole batch of malt is destroyed. Can you get your people down here? The two out here and the two in the house? I want to go check the kilns."

Gavan picked up his phone, ordering his security people to join them as soon as it connected. As he did that, she rushed into the barn with Drew right behind her. She stopped and rounded on him. "You have got to be joking. This is my home and my distillery, and Gavan is right out there."

"Yes, Mistress, and his instructions were not to let you out of my sight unless he was right next to you."

Shaking her head, she went into the control room, looked at the temperature controls, and verified they were set accurately. "I need to go up to my grandfather's study."

"I'm right behind you."

"He wasn't kidding about the five minutes in the loo, was he?"

"I don't know that I'd give you that long any place other than here or the castle."

"You are so not funny," she said, biting her lip to try to keep a straight face.

"Then why are you laughing?" he said with a goofy grin.

"Come on," she said and started to jog toward the house.

"They should be here in a few minutes," said Gavan. "I've got Dougal going through the video feed."

"Okay. I need to take a look at something in my grandfather's study, and Drew is coming with me."

They entered the house and headed straight for her destination.

"Blaise? What's going on?" asked Vera as she came down the stairs.

"The malt's been ruined. I need to check the equipment logs," she said, pushing past her. Blaise fired up the laptop computer and pulled up the electronic logs that kept a record of kiln temperature and moisture of the malted barley. "Sonofabitch! And don't you ever tell him I swore."

"My lips are sealed," said Drew.

Blaise sent the report to the printer and had it printed twice. "Come on, Drew. I want to show this to Gavan."

Together, she and Drew ran to join Gavan and the security crew who'd been on duty the night before. She handed Gavan the report.

"What am I looking at?" he asked.

"The report indicates that the kiln temperature was increased."

"I can see that, but don't you bring up the temperature slowly?"

"Yes, but the temp was increased steadily. See that spike?"

"An equipment malfunction?"

She shook her head. "No way. I also ran a report that would have shown any abnormalities. Someone deliberately cranked up the temp."

"You mean someone ruined the batch on purpose? Sabotage?"

"Has to be," Blaise said before turning to the security crew. "No offense, but you guys wouldn't know how to do that. Did you see anyone around the malt barns after we closed down for the day?"

"No. Your assistant got all pissy with me when I was checking all the buildings," answered the head of the detail, a man known as Jonah.

"When was that? Do you remember?" asked Gavan.

Jonah nodded. "Yes, Sir. About half past seven."

"Tommy was here at seven thirty? Last night?" When the man nodded, she turned to face Gavan. "There's no reason for him to be here other than he knew nobody but the security guys would be here. He knows I've moved up to Castle Cat-Sith and that Vera would be in Inverness. And Tommy never, and I mean never, puts in overtime. Ever. Skates in right before eight and leaves at five on the dot."

"Jonah, find Tommy and bring him to me."

"This is my distillery and my problem..."

"Only forty-nine percent. When I get done with my fifty-one percent of the little weasel, you can have what's left."

"And they say you aren't a generous man," quipped Blaise.

Jonah came running back. "His car's here, but he's gone, boss. We don't know if he went left or right. They're firing up the chopper. They're going up to look for him from overhead. We're going to split up and start making a systematic search. We'll find him and bring him back."

Gavan nodded. "Blaise, what do we need to do with the malt?"

"Like I said, it's ruined. It's been fried and the germination destroyed. All we can do now is clean up the mess."

"You show us where the shovels are and where to put it and we'll get it done," said one of the other security men.

"Thank you, but the rest of my people should be here anytime, and we can get it cleaned up."

"Don't they have their other jobs?" asked Gavan.

"Yes, but…"

"No, buts. Drew, escort your mistress up to the main house. As soon as your people get here, I'll get those who normally work in the malt barns to supervise my guys so they can get it cleaned out."

"Let me repeat: my distillery."

"I understand that and while I do own fifty-one percent, I am responsible for one hundred percent of you." He turned her toward the house and gave her ass a hard swat. "House, now. Drew, you're with her."

"Gav…"

"That makes ten, Blaise," he growled but relented.

"He hasn't tried to escape. He's here somewhere and he's got to know that if you haven't already, you'll figure it out eventually. I want you and Vera up in the house with armed guards, so I know you're safe. You're too important to me to lose."

"Fine. If I got five for momentary doubt this morning, you have to give me five back for even thinking you'll ever get rid of me."

Gavan stood staring at her, knowing that although she might submit to him completely in terms of sex and discipline, she would never be subservient or meek... and he was glad of it.

"Done."

"Come on, Drew. I think I'll get while the getting is good."

She kissed Gavan's still scowling face, dodged the swat he meant to give her, and headed for the house with Drew not two steps behind.

When they entered the kitchen, Blaise was a little surprised no one was there until she heard a nasty thunk as something struck Drew from behind. As the big man fell, she expected to see Tommy, but instead found herself looking into the eyes of the captain of the Fire and Rescue Service. It wasn't until her gaze travelled down that she saw the gun with what she supposed was a silencer in his hand.

"Back up or I finish him," he said menacingly.

"Okay, take it easy," she said backing away as instructed.

"Tommy! Get yer ass in here and tie this one up too."

When Tommy appeared, he saw Blaise and blanched. "I'm sorry, Blaise."

"Fuck sorry," growled Craig. "Here," he said, fishing a large hypodermic out of his pocket. "Hit him with this in the fleshy part of his neck, then tie him up."

"Why, Tommy?" she asked. She knew there had been times she had over-reacted to things and yelled at him but setting a fire and ruining the malt seemed a bit extreme even for Tommy's over-the-top personality.

"You're going to call that chopper back and get me all the money that's in your safe. Then you're going to walk me and Tommy out. You, me, the pilot, and Tommy are going to take a ride to the mainland and we're going to get away."

She shook her head. "Never happen. Even if I was willing to participate, Gavan's people would never allow you to take me."

"Then we'll kill you."

Just behind him in the window, the gray, cloudy day brightened as something shimmered and sparkled immediately before a large, black tiger burst through the panes of glass. Blaise stepped back out of the way as Gavan's enormous jaws closed on Craig's wrist, severing it completely from his arm.

Craig grabbed his arm trying to staunch the bleeding as Tommy charged the enormous beast with the hypodermic held over his head in order to stab Gavan and depress the plunger. Blaise didn't think twice, she grabbed the gun, aimed at Tommy's head and pulled the trigger, grateful her grandfather had taught her to shoot. Her former assistant crumbled to the ground. She spun around, thinking to take out Craig as well, but wasn't forced to as a hole appeared in his forehead and a bullet zinged past her, lodging in the wooden door frame. He too dropped like a stone as Gavan sprang between them. Craig's shooter was revealed as he hit the floor.

"I'll be damned. So, the legends are true," Vera whispered.

Gavan snarled and was surrounded by the shimmering light. Once more, the black tiger turned to human and he stood, proud and tall and boasting a massive hard-on.

Vera rolled her eyes and tossed him a kitchen towel. "Put that thing away before you hurt somebody with it. Nobody wants to see your junk."

"Not true," teased Blaise. "I like seeing his junk. I especially like seeing it as he's driving it in and out of me."

Gavan opened the back door and picked up his jeans, pulling them on before stepping back inside.

The men who'd been with him followed by Blaise's workers had come running at the sound of Vera's handgun going off. Needing space, Blaise pushed past him and stepped outside.

"We've got the situation under control. Everybody go back to work. I'll be down as soon as I can be so we can figure out what we're going to do next." Stepping back inside, Gavan crushed her to his chest, his mouth swooping down to claim hers in a savage kiss that left her breathless and wildly aroused.

"You two," he said, indicating she and Vera. "In the study now. The rest of you, check on the other guys."

"They've been drugged and tied up," said Vera, "but their vitals were strong and steady."

Gavan nodded. "Get them untied and make them comfortable. Then seal off the house and call the constabulary."

"Tommy is easy enough to explain, but not this guy," said Vera, indicating Craig.

Gavan smiled slowly. "What makes you think I'll need to explain anything? Somebody call Hamish and tell him what's happened, I need he and Dougal here. Then send the chopper after them. Ladies, I believe I told you I wanted you in the study."

Vera drew Blaise to her. "Best do as he says. Doms can be nasty pieces of work when you scare the shit out of them."

"Gavan wasn't afraid of Craig."

"If Craig had been pointing the gun at Gavan? You're right. Pointing the gun at you? That's another story all together. Come on."

They bypassed Craig's body and headed to the study. Unsure of what to say to Vera, Blaise opted to say nothing.

Finally, Vera broke the silence. "You and your grandfather knew?"

"Granda for years. Me just in the last few days. You can't tell anyone, Vera. You know what people would do."

"Optimize the military and capture him and all of his kind, most likely. You and he have nothing to fear from me."

"That's good to know," said Gavan as he joined them.

"How?" Vera asked.

"All kinds of legends about an ancient sorceress, a witch, a goddess bestowing the gift of shape shifting on four of her familiars: a black leopard, a black lion, a black sabretooth, and a black tiger."

"Ireland, England, Scotland, and Wales?" Vera asked. Gavan nodded. "So that's what binds you four." Gavan nodded again. "I guess that explains a lot."

"What?" said Blaise, confused.

"Four of the most powerful syndicates in the UK. They've always seemed to have some kind of alliance that bound them to each other. Origin and an enormous secret that could destroy them all would explain why it has stood the test of time."

"Aye," said Gavan, sitting down in the same wing-back he'd spanked Blaise in. He reached for her and drew her easily into his lap.

"I take it the local cops work for you?" Vera asked.

"Aye. We'll dispose of the bodies, and we can simply tell the distillery workers that they were behind the sabotage and were killed in the resulting firefight." Gavan rubbed his temples. "But we need to either find out why or come up with a reasonable explanation. See, this is the real reason I don't normally kill people; there's way too much hassle and the paperwork can be a bitch."

There was a knock on the study door. "Gavan, it's Dougal. Hamish said I should come talk to you."

"Come in."

Dougal stepped inside. "Blaise. Vera. Gavan, you asked me to look at the security footage for you. When I saw Craig skulking around the malt barn last night, I started digging into him. It seems he and Tommy have been gambling and living the high life when they're not on Skye and embezzling funds to cover their lavish lifestyle. They figured with Lachlan dying, there'd be an audit..."

"So they tried to cover their tracks," finished Vera.

"In other words, you went beyond the scope of what I asked you to do."

"If I overstepped…"

"You did," said Gavan, "but you have my thanks. Knowing that makes cleaning this mess up a whole lot easier. We'll get the bodies disposed of. Can you work with Hamish and the cops to concoct a plausible story? Your alpha would consider it a great favor."

Dougal's happiness was plain to see. "It would be my honor, Alpha. And may I offer my congratulations to you and your lady."

"You may. Now, go get your things out of that crappy apartment and ask Hamish to get you set up in a room where you can have some of your electronics that need to be secured. If we can get the immediate problem with Tommy and Craig handled, we'll figure out the rest next week."

"Yes, Alpha. Thank you."

Dougal turned to leave.

"And Dougal?" said Gavan. "We'll expect you at the Teine."

"Yes, Alpha," Dougal said, closing the door behind him before letting out a loud and jubilant whoop.

"That's another secret we're going to have to trust you with, Vera," said Blaise.

Both she and Gavan looked at her quizzically.

"That the badass head of the Galloglass Syndicate is really just a big patriarchal teddy bear."

"That's not much of a secret," said Vera. "Most everyone at the club already knows."

CHAPTER 24

Oidhche Teine
        Castle Cat-Sith
Isle of Skye, Scotland
One Month Later

Their wedding was to be on the Summer Solstice. Like Lachlan's celebration of life, there would be two events: one here at the castle and the other at the club. Blaise had been amazed at how quickly Gavan and his people had been able to concoct a story that had made sense and been accepted by everyone. The fact that Vera had worked with Dougal to get it done had surprised everyone at first, but eventually no one thought much of it.

Blaise paced the floor of their rooms. It had all happened so fast, and yet it seemed like they'd always been together, and she'd been raised as a tiger-shifter. Gavan had opted not to claim her on their first Teine together. There had been too much pent-up emotion, and her grief over her grandfather was still too fresh. Instead, he'd opted to see to her needs first. That didn't mean he didn't keep her close to his side and fuck her two or three times a day; it just meant he hadn't claimed her with a mating bite to start her transition.

Gavan walked out of the bath, his hair still wet from his shower. "We can wait another month if you aren't ready."

"No, I'm ready, and I want this Gavan, more than anything."

"I love you, *brèagha*."

She still thrilled when he told her that… and he told her that a lot.

"I love you too, Gavan."

He held out his hand to her. "Then come and be one with me."

Food and drink were plentiful at one of the clan's Teines. Their people enjoyed one another's company, and it was fascinating to watch them run and play as both tiger and human—shifting back and forth, seemingly at will. She'd been in enough clubs that nudity didn't bother her in the least, and she had just the tiniest bit of an exhibitionist in her.

Gavan had kept her primed and ready most of the day. Her nipples had been hard and distended and had ached anytime they weren't in his mouth. Her pussy had been dripping from either her own arousal, or his cum since early that morning. He hadn't exactly denied her orgasms. In fact, he'd supplied plenty of those, but he'd also ensured that she was in a highly aroused state for hours. She'd worn a loose silk shift that tied at the neck and fell to mid-calf with a deep slit up both sides. Gavan kept her either in his lap or close beside him, his hand always resting on her thigh and often slipping up under her dress to keep continual contact with her.

As the merriment continued to rise, Gavan stood, pulling her to her feet and tossing her over his shoulder.

"You can be a real neanderthal when you try."

"You're wrong, *brèagha*. I don't have to try at all."

He carried her into the darkness where the only light was provided by the full moon and starry sky. She could hear others making love in the distance. It was indistinct, but there was a kind of background accompaniment to the sharp snapping and crackling of the large bonfire.

Gavan had been attentive and loving all day, but she could sense the change in him. When he sank down into the sand, pulling her with him, he rucked up her dress and rendered her naked in the blink of an eye.

"Now, *brèagha*, I will make you one with me and the heavens above will hear you yowl."

He'd only been wearing his jeans, so stripping down to nothing took no time at all. Gavan pulled her beneath him, rolling her first onto her belly, then pulling her to her knees and moving behind her so that her lower legs were on either side of him as he knelt. Grasping her hips in order to ensure she couldn't move away from him, he drove his cock into her in a single hard lunge, making her cry out. No one had ever been able to make her come simply from the act of mounting her, but Gavan could and did almost every single time. There was something primal about the way he fucked. Dominant and possessive, his body called to her regardless of how many times he did it.

Blaise dug her hands into the sand as he began to thrust in and out with a hard, steady rhythm. Again and again, he pounded into her, groaning and growling as he did so. The growls were feral and primitive, and she responded to them on a visceral level. She tried to move with the same syncopated beat that he fucked her, but he wouldn't allow it. Her pussy convulsed along his length as she came a second time. Gavan dragged himself almost to the point where he was no longer inside her, only to drive back in deeper and more powerfully.

The second time she cried out, she could feel it unleash something in him. The thrusting became raw and wild, and her cries became screams as he hammered her pussy with ruthless intent. She could feel another orgasm threatening to send her into freefall as his hands brushed away her hair, baring the nape of her neck. With a primal roar that sent her reeling, sharp fangs, powered by skull crushing jaws bit down. Blaise screamed in surrender, pleasure, and pain as he finally claimed her. Renewed arousal and passion flared, sending heat and need through her entire system.

Between the savage bite and his painful grip, she couldn't move. All she could do was accept and yield, allowing him to make her one with him and complete the mating bond. He drew back again, but this time when he pushed forward, it was if raised nubs all along his cock scraped her inner walls, lighting her up like nothing ever had. It was far from painful, more like a rough, sensual tickling. She couldn't see what all the fuss was about; this new sensation was incredible. Before that thought could fully form, Gavan pulled back and she understood why he'd called them barbs and not nubs. She could feel them digging in, scoring her tender flesh before he thrust back in, replacing the pain with the sensual tickle. The barbs made themselves known once more as he dragged himself back. It was still painful, but the pain was beginning to morph into something she understood, sending pleasured spikes of ecstasy through her.

Gavan finally released her neck, replacing his mouth with his hand as he pressed down to force her upper body into the sand so he could fuck her harder and deeper. He stroked into her and this time when he pulled back, Blaise yowled. Her cry split the night, only to be answered by another.

Blaise realized that while she might be the only one being claimed this night, there were others all around her who were experiencing this same erotic session—part pure bliss and part rapture laced with pain. She yowled again, this time louder and more feral, and was answered by the roar of the man who'd claimed her as his own.

He continued pounding into her, his thrusts becoming more powerful and faster. There was no doubt in either of their minds who dominated and who submitted. Gavan completed her in a way she'd never thought possible. She came again and again, each climax more devastating in its intensity than the last. Finally, when she thought she had no more to give to appease his lust, he began to rumble in her ear, a sound that was part growl, part purr, and all Gavan.

"One more," he commanded as he fucked her with a zeal and fervor that she'd only known with him.

Instead of frightening her, her body responded, and her pussy trembled and quivered as he drove into her. His barbs continuing to ravage her sensitive flesh. Gavan's feral claiming of her had lit a wildfire that made the bonfire that burned so brightly further up the beach pale by comparison. At last, he drove into her, grinding his pelvis against her ass, forcing one last yowl from deep inside her as he drew back and the barbs dug in as his cum flooded her. The warm cream soothed her plundered pussy. When his cock had finally spewed its last drop, he kissed her shoulder and tipped them onto their sides.

Gavan held her close, stroking her body as he nuzzled and kissed her neck. His breathing was deep and even and she knew he was replete. She also knew that if the ability to shape-shift was his gift to her, the peace he found when they were fused together like this was hers to give to him. He whispered words of an ancient language that she didn't speak but that her heart could understand.

Blaise wasn't sure how long they lay together before Gavan stood, pulled on his jeans, and scooped her up in his arms, cradling her to his chest as he walked back toward the castle. She didn't know what the future would bring and didn't much care. As long as she shared it with this man, it was a pact she would hold to forever.

Thank you for reading. I hope you enjoyed meeting Blaise and Gavan. The next book in the Syndicate Masters series is The Agreement. *Are you ready to meet Joshua Knight, the Lion of London, and Peyton Cooper, the hard-hitting investigative journalist who wants to solve a brutal murder in which he seems to be involved?*

. . .

CLICK HERE TO PREORDER THE AGREEMENT NOW

And if you enjoyed THE PACT, you'll love the Ghost Cat Canyon series. The prequel novella Determined is FREE to download!

"Intense, exciting and fast paced." Reviewer

You never know what darkness lurks in the shadows. Don't miss the exciting new series, Masters of the Savoy, starting with ADVANCE! Can the Hero save his Creator or will it turn into another tragedy?

DOWNLOAD ADVANCE FOR FREE

I have some free bonus content for you! Sign up for my newsletter https://www.subscribepage.com/VIPlist22019. There is a special bonus scene, just for my subscribers. Signing up will also give you access to free books, plus let you hear about sales, exclusive previews and new releases first.

If you enjoyed this book we would love if you left a review, they make a huge difference for indie authors.

As always, my thanks to all of you for reading my books.

Take care of yourselves and each other.

FIRST LOOK

THE AGREEMENT

Peyton Cooper had been tossed out of more than one first-class office building in England's glittering capital of London, but never by two thugs. They were perfectly groomed and elegantly dressed, but no Saville Row tailor could truly cover the outline of a gun under a man's jacket.

"I'm going."

"Yes, you are," said the one she'd dubbed "Horace" because he reminded her of the short, bulky villain in the 1961 animated film, *101 Dalmatians*. Only this Horace's bulk came from muscle, not fat, but still the comparison seemed apt.

His partner, as in the film, was a long, lean goon she'd nicknamed Jasper. "Out you go, Ms. Cooper. You need to keep your nose out of other people's business, especially Mr. Knight's."

She was ushered outside, and the glass door was

firmly closed behind her. If Knight thought that would make her go away, he didn't know much about her brand of investigative reporting. Besides, it wasn't like she'd really seen anything. Sure, there'd been a naked girl kneeling between his legs giving him what had seemed to be an exceptional blow job, given the expression on his face, but how he spent his time was his business. But she had questions and he was the man who could give her answers, whether he liked it or not.

Peyton spent the next few hours perched on the wide ledge of the planters that flanked either side of the sweeping stairs that led into the building. She watched as people came and went through the sleek revolving door. She smiled as she remembered how she'd loved revolving doors as a child.

Knight came through the door amidst a goon squad of four: two in front, two in back, and Knight in the middle. She had to note that his guys were good. Knight himself moved with the predatory grace and skill of the beast he'd been compared to by so many, the black lion.

The first indication she had that there was anything amiss was when Knight spotted her a split second before shouting, "Down! Get down!" and broke free of his entourage to get to her.

He slammed into her body with the force of a freight train. Knight caught her around the waist and shoulders, pulling her down and rolling with her as several shots ricocheted off the granite that she'd been sitting on only minutes before. She could feel his breath being expelled violently as she fell on top of him, and he crushed her to his body then maneuvered her so that she was caught between Knight and the stone planter.

There had been a sort of delayed reaction between when Knight had hit her, and the bullets zinged past as the sounds of panic rose when people realized someone was shooting at them. *Can't be much of a sniper if he hit the planter instead of Knight.*

Books in this series
Syndicate Masters
The Bargain
The Pact
The Agreement
The Understanding

ABOUT DELTA JAMES

Other books by Delta James: https://www. deltajames.com/

As a USA Today bestselling romance author, Delta James aims to captivate readers with stories about complex heroines and the dominant alpha males who adore them. For Delta, romance is more than just a love story; it's a journey with challenges and thrills along the way.

After creating a second chapter for herself that was dramatically different than the first, Delta now resides in Virginia where she relaxes on warm summer evenings with her lovable pack of basset hounds as they watch the birds of prey soaring overhead and the fireflies dancing in the fading light. When not crafting fast-paced tales, she enjoys horseback riding, hiking, and white-water rafting.

Her readers mean the world to her, and Delta tries to interact personally to as many messages as she can. If you'd like to chat or discuss books, you can find Delta on Instagram, Facebook, and in her private reader group https://www.facebook.com/groups/348982795738444.

If you're looking for your next bingeable series, you can get a FREE story by joining her newsletter https://www.subscribepage.com/VIPlist22019.

The Bargain

The Pact

The Agreement

The Understanding

Masters of the Deep

Silent Predator

Fierce Predator

Savage Predator

Wicked Predator

Ghost Cat Canyon

Determined

Untamed

Bold

Fearless

Strong

Boxset

Tangled Vines

Corked

Uncorked

Decanted

Breathe

Full Bodied

Captured and Claimed

Made in the USA
Monee, IL
22 December 2022

23401314R00156